Also by Akiva Hersh
Boy in the Hole

To receive special offers, bonus content, info on new releases and, author updates visit akivahersh.com

THE MAGUS AND THE FOOL

Akiva Hersh

Copyright © 2022 by Akiva Hersh
All rights reserved.

No part of this book may be reproduced in any form or by any electronic or mechanical means, including information storage and retrieval systems, without permission in writing from the author except by a reviewer, who may quote brief passages in a review. Scanning, uploading, and electronic distribution of this book or the facilitation of such without the permission of the author is prohibited. Please purchase only authorized print editions, and do not participate in or encourage piracy of copyrighted materials. Your support of the author's rights is appreciated. Any member of educational institutions wishing to photocopy part or all of the work for classroom use, or anthology, should send inquiries to: akiva.hersh@gmail.com

LIBRARY OF CONGRESS
CATALOGING-IN-PUBLICATION DATA
Names Hersh, Akiva, author.
Title The Magus and The Fool / Akiva Hersh
Identifiers LCCN 2022901374 (print)
ISBN-13 979-8-9856515-1-5
Editor David Samuel Levinson
Design Coverkitchen
Author photo Christine Bazan-Hall

This book is a work of fiction. Names, characters, places, and incidents are the product of the author's imagination or are used fictitiously. Any resemblance to actual events, locales, or persons, living or dead, is coincidental.

Acknowledgements

I want to express my love to everyone who identifies as an LGBTQIA+ person. This book is for you. For us. Because we have all experienced those haters who dashed our dreams, and because we carry the weight of our false selves, dragging them from the past into the future. Still, we must carry on and learn to let them go.

To the allies of the LGBTQIA+ community, you make the world a better place. Now go forth and make disciples; we need more people like you.

I'm eternally grateful to my cousins Gene, Susan, Kristin, and my friend and confidant, Jayne. Without your love, guidance, and acceptance, I truly don't know who I would be.

And special thanks to Ryan Smith, who gave me valuable insights into the transgender experience. So much of your advice made it into this novel. Alas, some had to be cut out. Snip, snip!

Dedications

For Melanie, Steve, Ed, David, and Chana: the characters in this book may appear more like you than they are, fuckers!

And for my children, Shai and Nechama, whose lives are better stories than any book in the world.

And finally, for my mother, Sharon, may her memory be for a blessing. I think you would have really liked this one.

Except the heaven had come so near,
So seemed to choose my door,
The distance would not haunt me so;
I had not hoped before.
But just to hear the grace depart
I never thought to see,
Afflicts me with a double loss;
'T is lost, and lost to me.

Emily Dickinson

Ere the net is noticed by us,
Is a happier one imprison'd,
Whom we, one and all, together
Greet with envy and with blessings.

The Magic Net, by Johann Wolfgang von Goethe

Chapter One

When I was a boy and more eager to eavesdrop I overheard my father admonishing a dinner guest, saying, "Remember where you came from and know where you are going."

He never told me this advice directly as talking to each other was not our strongest suit. But his words impacted me. I'm careful not to leap to conclusions about people's motivations. His philosophy inspired me to view humanity with a voracious curiosity. Still, that fascination also made me prey to dull and pointless talk by those who abuse such a quality in a person. They sniff it out like a truffle pig. And so, in college, I was dubbed Mr. Diplomat because it got around that I could keep a secret, many of which my ears wish they had never heard. At the slightest hint that an unsolicited confession was heading my way, I complained of a headache and coughed uncontrollably before whichever of my classmates let loose upon me their derivative, affected drivel.

I have tried to heed my father's advice because it seemed sensible. But I am also an idealist, and I have failed to remain faithful to it, fearing that where I have been might occlude my vision of where I want to go. And yet this failure on my part reminds me that others are troubled by the same worry and I at least owe them the kindness of keeping an open mind. However, time and experience have taught me that my compassion is limited.

When I came back from Austin last fall, I craved a world that was even tenor, one emitting a singular pitch into which everyone was tuned. No longer did I want to face the riotous mob inside every human heart. But then there was Oskar Jacobi, the only person I didn't want to integrate into this harmonious world. Jacobi remained the phantom of my hatred. If the ego is born by the universal stream of consciousness rushing into individual minds, then Jacobi was magnificent. His mind was calibrated to detect the best life had to offer in the way radar transmits signals into the sky to detect far-off weather formations. He had been gifted with a sensitivity for optimism and passion like no one I had ever encountered, and I never hope to again. With Jacobi, everything turned out just as it should have. But no matter what the blessings were that came with his gift, the curses hung in the air like smoke in the burning aftermath of his dreams. He is the reason why I have no tolerance for the passion and heartbreak of men.

* * *

The Iversons have been in Oberlin, Ohio, nearly since the foundation. We are a middle-class bunch, some of us professors, others hardworking in various businesses, including the town's newspaper. But I sometimes wonder if I weren't adopted, as I bear little resemblance to my forefathers with crooked noses and overgrown, wavy beards. I did inherit their diligence regarding money and education, however, and graduated from Oberlin College in 2019. My father attended and taught at Oberlin, as did my grandfather.

I became anxious and ill at ease with the Midwestern pace of life. Time trickled by like the creek that snuck through the town as if it were an apology. I decided to move to Austin, Texas and accepted a position with a watchdog firm whose mission was to hold big businesses accountable. My family considered my plans and gave me a cautious but supportive green light.

Dad thought it was such a worthy thing he agreed to loan me enough money to live on for a year. With some ambivalence, I left Oberlin for my new life in the spring of 2021.

I should have gone with my first instinct and rented a room in the heart of Austin, but a charismatic young colleague from the office convinced me we should rent a cottage together on Lake Travis. Our commute would only be forty minutes, and he was nice to look at. We found a rental, a rustic relic from the sixties, but right before we moved in, the firm sent him to Florida so, I went to the lake on my own. I had my clothes, a cat named Achilles, and a late model Nissan SUV.

For a few days, I felt like the new kid in school with no one to sit with at lunch. Then one afternoon, a man, quite the hippie, who had just moved in near me, hailed me at my mailbox.

"Hey, dude, how do you get to the market here on Emerald Bluff?"

After I gave him directions, I wasn't a newcomer anymore. I felt ownership of and power in this parcel by the lake.

Summer burst in with golden shards of sunlight ricocheting across the surface of the water. The gentle green hills surrounding the bluff seemed to move on a separate trajectory from the lake and the blue sky. Pontoon boats dotted the water, and people swam, and there was movement everywhere. Life was renewed in the month of June.

I had so much research to get done. I was preparing for an upcoming campaign against a bill that would endanger Texans' right to organized protest and needed to read everything about the issue and then write campaign proposals for email and web publications. But the cool water and the warm sun, a contrast that gave me great pleasure, was a tempting distraction.

I had been a bit of a writer at Oberlin and many of my editorials were published in *The Oberlin Review*, but to resurrect those skills now felt like I was being diminished as if I were going backward rather than forward. On our infrequent phone calls, Dad reminded me that integrating the new experiences the world offered with what was already manifest in me was a characteristic of wisdom. It wasn't bad advice, for we should mine the depths of past experiences and store whatever resources we get from them for the future.

I couldn't have known before I moved into that cottage that I'd stumbled upon one of the strangest places in the United States, heralding its own slogan, *Keep Austin Weird*, which the raucous lake community heartily embraced. The peninsula of Emerald Bluff juts out into the winding Colorado River, looking like a foot about to step on a snake. East of there, across the river, is a clothing-optional beach where anyone can flash breasts and asses before admiring eyes. Police boats patrol the waters and stop drunken boaters for swerving and speeding. Due north of me sits The Hollows, a crescent-shaped section of the mainland, with rugged cliffs and rocky beaches. Perhaps the two were one before the Colorado River tore them apart.

I lived on Emerald Bluff which was more casual than The Hollows. Although casual fails to describe the stark and mischievous differences between the two. My house sat at the very northern edge of the bluff, just a few minutes' walk to the cove. On either side of me were elephantine homes worth millions. The one on my right was a mammoth marvel by the most decadent standard—a recently built three-story mansion. It was crowned by a half-circle foyer, eight fireplaces, a grand staircase, two swimming pools (one fresh, one saltwater), and three acres of landscaped native grasses, shrubs, and gardens. This was Jacobi's estate, although I didn't know it at the time. My cottage, a small blight on the landscape, was in an underdeveloped section of Emerald Bluff, so I had quite a view of the lake, a partially obstructed view of Jacobi's central garden, and the comfortable presence of billionaires.

Across the river from me glared the limestone-bricked palatial fortresses of the ever-chic Hollows. I consider the beginning of my life in Austin the night I went over there to have dinner with Donovan and Fallon Macandeior. Donovan was my cousin, and I had attended Oberlin with his wife, Fallon.

Besides her academic accomplishments at Oberlin, Fallon had earned the reputation for being the single most frightening woman to piss off on campus. Her family was ridiculously rich—earning her scorn from everyone for the way she was frivolous with her wealth. Her propensity to spend money rendered one speechless: for example, she'd bought a harras of Akhal-Teke horses just so she and her friends might ride dressage, which they never did. I had never met anyone close to my age who had enough money to do that.

They had lived in Rome for some time so Fallon could expand her business. Then for no apparent reason, they decided on Austin as "our forever home," said Donovan over FaceTime one night many months ago. But was it really? I had no clue how Donovan truly felt about it. Still, I couldn't imagine Fallon trading the down-home feel of Lake Travis for the drama of acquiring a flailing company, gutting its weakest employees, and turning it into a thriving revenue stream.

And so, in the half-light of that warm, still evening, I drove to The Hollows to dine with the only people I knew in Austin but barely knew at all. Their mansion was more elegant than I could have possibly imagined, a modern but comfy waterfront property constructed of natural materials—quarried limestone, fir beam ceilings, clerestory, and wall-to-wall windows that welcomed natural light for an airy ambiance. It had a gourmet kitchen, a separate guest house and office, an outdoor spa, pool, and fire pits. Their sloped lawn swelled up from the beach and spread itself out another hundred yards, where it finally caressed the house and opened its unflinching palm to perch it on the overlook. A warm, lazy breeze pawed my face and made its way, catlike, through the open windows. Fallon Macandeior, in skin-tight jodhpurs, sat wide-legged on a bench and watched me approach the portico.

She hadn't changed at all since our days at Oberlin. She was masculine, all sharp thin lines contrasted by shadow and light, a chiaroscuro of a woman. Her copper-like eyes shone out of her deep sockets and complimented her threatening appearance. She was slender and muscular, and she possessed every inch of her clean and crisp breeches. Hers was a body made for war—a harsh and severe form. One could pick out her bourbon-throated voice in a roaring crowd at the races. Her tone conveyed disapproval, even when she was pleased. We got along fine at Oberlin, but I never knew where I stood with her.

"I'm sure you've never stepped foot in a more fantastic house than this," she said, her metallic eyes darting about my face like a searchlight.

She grasped my arm and directed my gaze toward the lake with her long pinkie finger, her French manicured nail cut across the horizon. "One of the Pickens' boys owned all this until he lost it in a scandal, poor bastard." Fallon pushed the small of my back toward the entrance, her style of hospitality. "Come in."

We walked into a luminous foyer. The wood, stone, and tile gave one a sturdy feeling, but the space was not constricting. The house was lined with windows, occasionally interrupted by a limestone wall. There were no curtains. The open windows drew a breeze into the house as if it were breathing. The kitchen and sitting room were practically one space, only separated by a counter and a thick wooden support beam. Vintage prints by Razzia and Gruau added alluring red and yellow colors to the spartan white limestone walls. Beneath the Bugatti Atlantic poster sat a prodigious chalky-white couch where two men were submerged on the plush cushions like blackberries on a dollop of whipped cream. They were both dressed in black, and the top buttons of their shirts were open wide, exposing bronze skin over collar bones that begged attention. I became aware that I was lingering on them well beyond polite social convention when Fallon Macandeior cleared her throat and pressed a button on the wall, and all of the windows slid closed with a crisp snap. The breeze vanished, and without it, the room's air became heavy and solid.

I did not know the smaller of the two men. He was stretched out with his legs crisscrossed on the dark leather ottoman, his manner dégagé. His face was turned up as though he were watching for something to fall from the ceiling. He did not acknowledge me at all.

The other man, Donovan, tried to push himself up off the couch and then giggled, and I laughed too, walking toward him.

"I can't stand it, cousin. I'm so happy to see you," said Donovan.

He laughed harder and took my hand. His face seemed to say that I was the most important person in the room to him. That was his way. He whispered something to me. I leaned in closer, and he whispered again that the benign man's last name was Safran.

Mr. Safran lowered his head to wink at me and then tilted his head back again, still waiting for whatever he was looking at to surely fall. I felt guilty for disrupting his watch, and I nearly apologized. I find self-absorption in others an undesirable trait, but rather than condemn them, I censure myself. So, I sought refuge in my cousin who had suddenly become an arsenal of questions. His speech was giddy, and he had the kind of voice that might make a dog tilt its head, trying to parse the words it could not understand. Donovan's face was eager and bright, like a stately fir decorated for Christmas. His eyes shone like silver ornaments. His full lips were shiny garlands, and his voice had a provocative quality that made you feel as if something extraordinary were about to happen.

I told him all about the family back home.

"How much do they miss me?" he asked, clasping his hands together like a child about to receive a gift.

"Everyone is sitting shiva. All the mirrors are draped in cloth, and no one eats anything but eggs."

"Fabulous! Fallon, let's visit Oberlin soon." Then as if the notion somehow connected, "Carry, my love, you have to see our little bundle of joy."

"Well, show me."

"My God, he's a toddler. And you've never seen him, you bore. He's sleeping anyway."

"Can't I just take a peek?"

"You've waited this long, Carry Iverson so another hour won't—"

Fallon Macandeior had been sulking near the counter. She strutted across the room and pinched my neck.

"Where are you working now, Carry?"

"I'm a campaign manager for a watchdog firm."

"Christ, of course, you are. Which one?"

"Greater Together."

"They can't be that great. I've never heard of them."

"You should be grateful for that. But stay in Austin long enough, and you'll hear about us."

"Long enough? Is that a challenge?" she asked, glaring at Donovan and then inching closer to my face. "Where the fuck else would I live, Carry?"

It was here that Mr. Safran sat up and said, "Serve that tea, hunty!" I was too stunned to realize that this was the first time he had spoken since I arrived. He inched his hips off the couch and stood.

"I'm hard as a corpse, and not in a good way. I've been vegging here too long."

"Whose fault is that?" Donovan said. "I've tried to get you to go into Austin with me all day."

"And do what? Boy watch? Shop for something your wife *doesn't* own? I'll pass," said Mr. Safran to no one but the chilled martini glistening in front of him. "I gotta werk. And thank you, Fallon dear, for the drink."

Donovan's cheeks flattened, and he stuck out his lips.

"You? Work?" Fallon slurped her cocktail like a cow at a stock tank.

I wondered where it was that Mr. Safran "werked." It was a pleasure to look at him. He was slim, with a boyish chest and face, and a spectacular posture which he highlighted by keeping his head in line with his shoulders. His silver-gray eyes glinted like polished hematite. He observed me with those eyes with a diplomatic grace.

"So you're over *there* on Emerald Bluff," he said, his tone underlining the separateness of our respective locales. "I know someone else who lives there."

"Do you?" I cleared my throat to swallow the rising inadequacy. "I just moved here. I don't know anyone, really."

"Darling, you *have* to know Jacobi."

"Jacobi?" said Donovan, startled. "Which Jacobi?"

Fallon interrupted to inform us the staff was ready to serve dinner. She locked her arm around mine and flexed her muscle, nearly dragging me from the sitting room in the way soldiers carry their wounded off the battlefield. The two men followed us, also arm in arm, out to a stone-paved deck surrounded by gravel, oak trees, soft white loungers, and a hand-carved table next to a flaming fire pit.

"Who lit the fire?" Donovan asked, nose wrinkled. He told one of the staff to turn it off. "The hottest days of the summer are here." Disgust left his face as quickly as the fire went out. "Don't you just bitch about the hottest days and then want them right back at the first freeze?"

"When did you quit enjoying winter?" I asked.

"I miss the snow, but I can do without the cold." I caught Donovan flashing his eyes at Fallon just then.

"Girls, we need to do something while I'm here." Mr. Safran held his head in his hands as if the world suddenly stopped spinning.

"Yes, we do," said Donovan. The white candle on the table appeared dim compared to his radiant face. "Like what? Any ideas?" He turned to me for input. "What would you like to do, Carry, since you're finally in Austin?"

Donovan gasped. "Oh my god, my hand is bruised."

All of us inspected his hand dutifully.

"Fallon, you really hurt me," he said. "Even if it was an accident, now I'm all black and blue. Guess those are the dues for marrying a cunning, unique, nervy, and talented—"

"Do not use cunning when talking about me," Fallon said with one hand on her hip. Her long finger jabbed at Donovan. "Even if you're being playful. Got it?"

"Cunning," repeated Donovan, giving Fallon a half-smile.

Donovan and Mr. Safran talked over each other during dinner, producing a counterpoint of melodies and harmonies with varying rhythms and tempos. It was not off-putting in the least. The rapport between them, a giddy-eyed, choreographed flirtation, was expansive enough for Fallon and me to feel included, even entertained now and then.

"I feel like a savage around you now, Donovan." Perhaps the third glass of Shiraz acted on me like a truth serum. "Don't you remember anything about farming or playing corn hole?"

"That was a different life," he said. "Our circle is a mélange of chichi classist twits who would be mortified by corn hole."

I was just toying with him, but Fallon found her soapbox and went with it.

"We're losing our goddamn society thanks to mindless people like that. Groups like Black Lives Matter, the Men's Rights movement, Arab Springs, for fuck's sake! We *all* matter. Have you heard of the Aryan Renaissance Society?"

"No, Fallon, I haven't. And I wouldn't."

"You should look into it, Iverson. You're an Oberlin man. You should be on top of these social issues. Greater Together, isn't that right?"

"I think Fallon has lost the plot. And when she's drunk," said Donovan, grief washing over his face, "she becomes much more expressive with her ideas," and then his voice trailed off.

"The theories are sound. They're backed by science and research," Fallon shot back. She crossed her arms and tapped her finger on her elbow. "Groups like the ARS have figured out how to keep things balanced. I'm not suggesting we do a repeat of Germany, fuck forbid."

"So what? We control the non-whites by passing oppressive laws?" countered Donovan.

"You need to get out more, Fallon, and stop throwing shade. Air out that brain a little, honey," said Mr. Safran.

Fallon leaned hard on the table. "Our people came from Vikings. Well, all of us except *you*, Safran."

Mr. Safran winked at me. (Here is as good a place as any to mention that Donovan was born an Iverson, of course. But Fallon insisted he take her last name, which was a boost for him all the way around.)

"If it weren't for the Vikings, we wouldn't have the fine arts, mathematics, the foundations of society. *We* have to maintain the balance," Fallon said.

The slender warrior-queen had morphed into an ogre before my eyes. She turned my stomach. I was about to launch into a full-on debate when the butler told her she had a call waiting in the office. She shoved her chair from the table with a huff and went inside, the butler trailing her. Fallon's departure freed something inside Donovan, and he leaned his face toward me, our cheeks almost pressing. "I deeply love having you at this table right now, Carry. You're a cherub, a total cherub. Isn't he?" He leaned into Mr. Safran. "A totally handsome cherub?"

I wanted to renounce what he'd said. No part of me was cherubic. He was inventing praise out of thin air. Maybe it was the wine. Perhaps it was the stress from Fallon's racist homily. Whatever it was, something else moved him.

"Do you want to hear a secret about the butler?" Donovan asked.

"That's why I came tonight."

"Well, he wasn't always a butler. He used to be a psychic to celebrities in LA."

"Here comes the really sad part," said Mr. Safran.

"He was doing very well for himself until he gave one of his clients the bad news."

"What was the bad news?" I asked.

"The client drew a card from his tarot deck, and he told her she would lose everything: her husband, her lover, and all of her wealth. She put the word out that he was a fraud, and he never did a reading for that crowd again."

I held back a laugh. Mr. Safran put a hand on my shoulder.

"Be careful what you laugh at, darling. The butler can still read."

"That's a great idea," said Donovan, calling the butler over. "My cousin here would love it if you gave him a reading."

The butler stiffened his shoulders. "Is now the right time, sir?"

"Please, go get your cards."

He returned with a black wooden box. Donovan gestured for him to sit.

"Just a short reading, then. From the Major Arcana. Your name, sir?"

"Carry." I tried to turn the smirk on my face into a polite smile.

"Please, think of a question and shuffle the deck."

He scattered the cards onto a silk scarf and watched me. I moved them around aggressively, and then he collected them into a neat rectangle.

"Now, cut the deck in half, and I will lay down three cards."

The images made no sense to me, but the butler rubbed his nose and took a deep breath.

"I'm suspicious of The Fool and The Magician in this reading. Please indulge me and reshuffle the deck."

I repeated the shuffle and cut the deck. His mouth fell open, and his eyes were wide.

"This is quite unusual."

"What do they mean?" I asked.

Mr. Safran lit two cigarettes and handed one to Donovan.

"The Fool was upright after the first shuffle. Now it's reversed but in the same place, next to The Magician which has also now been reversed. And then we have The Hermit."

"I think you fucked," said Mr. Safran, which irritated me.

"The Fool in this position indicates where you have come from, your recent past. When it is upside down, it can mean that you haven't paid attention to your instincts and have held back from taking a chance on someone or something."

"Okay. That's general enough I could plug any experience into that."

"Cousin," Donovan said. "Relax. Keep an open mind."

The butler cleared his throat. "The card in the next position shows something coming in your future. The Magician could be a man or a woman, or even yourself. Notice his wand is drawing power from above, directed to his outstretched hand pointing to the earth. But this one, too, is reversed."

"Meaning?"

"It most likely shows someone in your immediate future who abuses power and is blinded by fantasies. It's a warning about getting too close."

"Guilty!" Mr. Safran said, laughing. "Stay away from me, honey."

"And the last card?"

"The Hermit represents the most probable outcome. He is also reversed, which is of some concern."

"Why's that?"

"Notice all three of the cards have wands. The Hermit's wand is like a crutch, signifying the need for self-awareness. He also represents a withdrawal from society after a transition. But because he is reversed, it could mean an unhealthy withdrawal full of bitterness and distrust."

Fallon yelled for the butler from inside. Then she started yelling into the phone.

Donovan suddenly sat his glass down hard enough to startle the butler. They both got up and marched inside.

I looked at Mr. Safran for an explanation. He glanced at me with empty eyes. "So, what do you think—"

"Sha!" Mr. Safran silenced me. A quiet but ardent conversation took place in the office facing the patio. Mr. Safran leaned back in his chair toward the direction of the confrontation. Fallon and Donovan's volleys were like barking dogs, first muted and distant, then close and threatening. After a bit of silence, they started up again.

I cleared my throat. "So this Mr. Jacobi you mentioned—"

"Shut up, darling. I want to hear what's going on."

"Going on? What do you mean?"

"Oh, you don't know?" asked Mr. Safran. "All of Austin knows."

"Knows what?"

"Everyone knows that Fallon has a boy toy."

"A boy toy?" I parroted back.

Mr. Safran nodded like a bobblehead.

"You'd think that sugar baby would know not to call her during dinner!"

The revelation hadn't begun to sink in before there was the crunch of gravel, and Fallon and Donovan took their seats.

"Ah, when duty calls!" said Donovan, voice strained.

He scanned Mr. Safran and then me. "Even though the sun has set, it's still a gorgeous night. I think I even saw a cauldron of bats just over there near the beach. It's a gorgeous night, isn't it, Fallon?"

"Fucking gorgeous," she said.

"The butler gave Carry a reading. Do you want to hear what he said? It sounds—"

"It sounds like bullshit. Iverson, after dinner, you and I are going down to the stables."

The phone rang again. It shook us all like a peal of thunder. Donovan's chest caved, and the color left his face, as did the idea of the stables or any more talk about the tarot cards. As I was trying to put together the pieces of the puzzle I'd gathered that evening, I noticed the fire pit had been re-lit. But why? I wanted to look away from it, but I didn't want to see everyone so plainly. What was going through Fallon and Donovan's minds? I was able to steal a glance at Mr. Safran who was fingering the rim of his glass with his pinkie. Not even he, worldly Mr. Safran, could ignore this clanging intrusion into our affair. Had this not involved Donovan, I might have been amused—but my hand remained near the phone in my pocket should there be an emergency.

Fallon walked back into the house. Mr. Safran followed several steps behind her. Donovan and I walked side by side, unhurried, as though we were approaching something we wanted to avoid. We stopped at the porch on the side of the house and sat down on an iron-work settee.

Donovan ran his fingers over the stubble on his face. His eyes came to rest on the dark lake.

"You know, Carry, for cousins, you and I are almost strangers. How many events in my life have you missed? The wedding. The birth of my son."

"I went through some hard times after I graduated from Oberlin."

"Well, my life has been shit, and that's the truth."

If the intrusion tonight was any indication, who could argue with him? I retreated to safer territory. "So, how is the little one? Eating well and all that?"

"Of course." He kept his eyes on the lake, speaking into the darkness. "Should I tell you what came out of my mouth when he was born?"

"If you want."

"It's quite revealing, Carry. Goes to my state of mind. Fallon wouldn't allow me in the room for the birth, said it was undignified. Hours later, I found a nurse and asked him if I had a son or a daughter. He said it was a boy, and I cried. Hard. Do you know why I cried?"

"The overwhelming joy?" I guessed.

Donovan blew something out of his mouth, part laughter and part disgust. "No. I cried because I let go of any hope I had for him in this world then and there. Best case, he turns out to be a handsome, charming idiot because that's what men are expected to be. Worst case, he becomes something like me. The world is a shitty place, and everyone knows it."

"But Donovan, what about—"

"Carry, I love you, but you're so provincial. I've been around the world and I never discovered anything new." He sneered, giving me a look that reminded me of Fallon. "I'm so god damned cultured, aren't I?"

He quit speaking. I knew what he was saying was a lie. But his confession—hell, the entire dinner affair—seemed to be a conspiracy to trap me into some cult. My stomach rolled as though something black and earthy needed to be let out. At that moment, his beautiful face darkened, and he leered at me in the way a con knows he has duped his mark.

***

Mr. Safran and Fallon were in the large living room at the far end of the house. Safran was sitting with his back to the fire, leafing through a photo book about Louis Vuitton. Fallon was standing at the large window tinkering with a high-tech telescope, the reflection of the flames dancing across its sleek, white surface.

When we crossed the room to sit next to Mr. Safran, he slammed the book shut and set it on the sofa next to him, and bolted upright in one motion.

"It's late, and this bad boy needs his beauty sleep."

"Levi has a match tomorrow," said Donovan. "He's gearing up for the world championship."

"What sort of championship?" I asked.

"Levi has his blackbelt in Krav Maga." Donovan made a chopping gesture through the air. "He almost won the junior championship a few years ago."

"Well, off to bed for me, darlings. Sweet dreams, Mr. Iverson. See you when I see you."

Levi looked back at me over his shoulder. He lingered a little too long, the way a politician stared you down until he's sure he's won your vote.

"But, of course, you'll see him. And often. The two of you will be best of friends, kikis, even if I have to force you both."

"What's that, Don? You're slurring your words. Bye, Felicia," Mr. Safran said to him, slinking his hand up the stair rail.

"Safran is a good person," said Fallon. "But they shouldn't let him roam so freely."

"Who shouldn't?" asked Donovan.

"Don't be dense."

"His family has all but a foot in the crypt already. What do they know? Anyway, I think Carry and Levi will spend a lot of time together out here this summer. And the lake and the sun will do them both some good."

Donovan and Fallon assessed each other quickly and silently. I thought I saw them nod.

"Is he from Austin?" I blurted out.

"Columbus, Ohio. We shared our fabulous childhood together there."

"Did you bring Carry around on that subject?" asked Fallon.

"Oh, on the porch, darling? Yes, I pounded him hard about the superiority of the Vikings and all that."

"It went in one ear and out the other," I said. They walked me to the driveway and held hands in some sort of perverse complicity. When I started up my SUV, Donovan waved his hands and yelled, "Wait, Carry! I have to ask you something. Fallon and I heard that you had gotten serious with a boy back home."

"Oh, yeah, we did hear that. It was almost an engagement, was it not?" asked Fallon.

"It's all rumors."

"No, we heard it from all around. There has to be a nugget of truth in it," said Donovan.

You can leave your state, but you can never leave social media. I won't quit a relationship because of gossip, but I would not let rumors define me. It was nothing like an engagement. As an institution, I objected to marriage and its Judeo-Christian origins. As an idea, well, I didn't consider myself the marrying type.

But their curiosity about me made me feel like I mattered to them and made them seem less untouchable. As I drove home, though, I felt more confused about the night's revelations. Why didn't Donovan just leave her? That was more puzzling than Fallon bedding a boy in Austin. Obviously, the monotony of motherhood had already set in, and she was starving for something more virile to control.

When I arrived back at my cottage on Emerald Bluff, I parked the SUV and sat in the yard. An owl hooted nearby. Achilles' silhouette moved across the front window; he was probably hungry. I thought I'd seen a meteor flash right to left across the sky, and it was then I felt another presence. Pale from the moonlight, he was like an apparition stepping out of the shadow of his mansion. He was watching the sky as well. He slipped his hands into his pockets and took a step, soundless, secure. It was Jacobi.

Since Mr. Safran had brought him up at dinner, I figured this was a low-key way to introduce myself. But I stopped. He looked so comfortable there by himself. And then he stretched his hand out toward the black lake. His fingers shook. I looked in the direction where he was reaching but saw nothing except the luminescent fountain on the Macandeior's hill. I had seen it earlier from up close. The wide basin was Italian marble, and in polished copper, Apollo, facing east, rises from the water to greet the new morning in his chariot drawn by four horses. Cherubs herald his arrival with trumpets. A single spout of water, illuminated by white lights, shoots several feet into the air. When I turned back to Jacobi, he was gone, and it was me who was alone in the restless dark.

Foolishness is indeed the sister of wickedness.

Sophocles

Chapter Two

The Colorado River winds its way southeast from Emerald Bluff to the heart of Austin, where it is called Lady Bird Lake (it loses the former First Lady's moniker after passing under the interstate through East Austin). Just blocks from the Capitol Building, among the bars, the restaurants, and the upper-class shops, stands an unremarkable six-story bell tower on the bank of the river. Tourists and locals rarely give it a second look. It was built in 1930 and was styled after the Italianate campaniles. The bell tower was used to train firefighters and provide public demonstrations of the department's firefighting power. Now its red-brown bricks are charred from fire damage and age. But the bells still chime the hour and clang out Christmas carols for those close enough to hear them. This is a relic from a forgotten time. You might say the entire area around it is, too, for the homeless camps moved in—there are hundreds of makeshift tents clustered around the tower—and joggers, walkers, pet lovers, rowers, and business people pass just close enough to see the squalor but are still plenty of distance away to ignore it. If anyone were to take note of the area, they would see the drooping, dreary gray tarps rippling in the wind. And bicycles, and discarded office chairs, and tattered umbrellas, treasures of the displaced.

And overlooking the tower is a twelve-story boutique hotel with a restaurant and jazz club. On its west side is a multi-colored mural. The face is feminine. Her collagen-inflated lips are parted. Her eyes are an entire story tall. Wonder Woman rises out of her brain, holding broken chains in each hand. On one side of the woman's cheek, against a red background, the word

EQUALITY is limned vertically in orange, spanning three floors. The Giantess was meant to send a message that anyone can be who they want to be.

Congress Avenue Bridge juts out from the shore between the bell tower and the Giantess. Waiting commuters are able to observe the sad spectacle during rush hour, just long enough to ponder the ironic juxtaposition. It was in this area where I encountered Fallon Macandeior's boy toy.

She had seen to it to make the affair as public as possible. Her friends were in a huff over the way she flaunted him in the clubs and the coffeehouses and displayed him in restaurant booths, as though he were a floral centerpiece while she schmoozed with anyone who might end up owing her a favor.

Curiosity got the best of me and, forgetting the hurt Donovan was in, I went with Fallon into Austin one afternoon. We were stopped at the traffic light at the bell tower just yards away from the Giantess's demanding stare when Fallon turned to me and told me our destination was just up ahead.

"You'll be glad you decided to come," she said.

I had made no such decision. Fallon helped herself (often) to the bourbon at lunch and then said, "Since your afternoon is free, Carry, let's go for a drive." It was a compulsory choice.

We parked at an industrial building next to a rundown motel. How this establishment was still around remained a mystery. We were blocks from the convention center, the Four Seasons, and a Marriott. And decaying in this forsaken plot of land was a rusting metal-sided structure divided into three. The first third, the part closest to us, was for rent, the middle third a hair and nail salon, and the final third a tiny motel with a dingy sign: *The Titan. Hourly, nightly, and weekly rates.*

I followed Fallon through a sliding metal door and sidestepped a giant spider web. The only art on the wall was a framed sign that read:

> URINATING DEFECATING OR SPITTING IS
> A BIG HEALTH CONCERN AND IS STRICTLY
> PROHIBITED IN THE LOBBY. MGMT.

The smell of burnt coffee and hairspray slithered into the lobby from the connecting door to the salon.

"Shyla, darling, you busy?" yelled Fallon, tapping away at the silver service bell on the counter.

I heard a doorknob getting worked over by a key. Suddenly a large woman waddled over to us. She looked to be in her thirties if I'm being generous.

"Getting many new clients?" asked Fallon, trying to embrace the woman.

"They're coming. Summer's just slow."

"Well, I'd have thought it would be the opposite. Look, Shyla, if the salon isn't working out for you, I can sell it—"

"No, ma'am, I don't mean that. We're gonna do better."

"Anyway, I want to set an appointment for next week."

"You couldn't have just called?" asked Shyla, looking as if the left side of her face had had an accident with her right.

"We were in the area," said Fallon.

A tan, blonde man in his early thirties appeared behind the plexiglass window. He wiped his hands across his nose. He was good-looking in the way rough trade could be; his arms were chiseled, and his chest was so large his shirt strained at the button. He waved, walked around the counter ignoring his wife, and kissed Fallon's hand. She licked her lips.

"Shyla, get us all something cold to drink. It's a hot one today."

"Yes, Mrs. Macandeior," she said, tottering off into the salon.

Fallon pinched the man's nipple while pointing at me. "Liam Kearns, Carry Iverson. He's nothing to worry about. He's family, and besides, he's queer."

Liam twitched free, still wincing, and managed a nod in my direction.

"You and I are fucking today," said Fallon. "Uber over to the tavern. I'll meet you there."

"What about him?" he asked.

"I have plans for Carry."

She made for the door just as Shyla Kearns returned, nonplussed, a tray and four styrofoam cups in her hands.

We pulled into a country-style tavern and waited in the car for Liam. It was a few days before the Fourth of July, and a skinny Latino boy scribbled letters in the air with a sparkler.

"What a shit hole," said Fallon.

"At least it has a salon," I said with a grin.

"It's the only way to get him out of this place. He doesn't belong here."

"Doesn't his wife get suspicious?"

"Shyla? She thinks he goes to visit family in North Austin. Besides, she's a hermit and prefers to be alone."

So Fallon and her boy toy and I drove back downtown. He had changed his clothes and was now wearing a white linen shirt, tight jeans, and a pair of espadrilles, all purchased by Fallon, for sure. The light of the sun began to shift from white-yellow to orange. We zipped past a row of tall buildings when Liam let out a gasp. Fallon hit the brakes.

"I *gotta* have one of those," Liam said, tapping on his window. "The apartment needs—a dog."

We reversed and parked next to a man who ridiculously resembled Richard Simmons. He had at least a dozen pups in a cardboard box.

"What kind of dogs are they?" asked Liam.

"What kind do you want them to be, mister?"

"I want one of those service dogs, the kind you can take into restaurants; you have that kind?"

The man raised his eyebrows and flicked something from his nostril. He made a diligent show of sorting the puppies in the box. Finally, he picked one up, its tail wagging.

"That's just a mutt," said Fallon.

"It's more of a terrier, ma'am." He stroked the dog's wiry coat. "It's hypoallergenic."

"Adorable," said Liam. "How much?"

"This one here? It'll be a hundred dollars, on account of it being hypo—"

"Take this." Fallon thrust a wad of cash at the man, far more than one hundred dollars. "Now feed them properly."

The terrier nestled into Liam's lap. He kissed and petted the dog more freely than a typical dog, I thought, because he must have believed he wouldn't be allergic to it.

"But I have to know. Is it a boy or a girl?"

"It's a bitch," said Fallon, and she punched the gas.

We cut across Fifth Street, nearly empty on a Sunday afternoon, and slowed down in front of a newly built luxury highrise a few blocks from the governor's mansion.

"Wait," I said. Drop me here so you two can—"

"The hell I will," imposed Fallon. "You'll hurt Liam's feelings if you don't come up to our apartment. Right, Liam?"

"Yeah, man! It's awesome up there. And I'll text my brother. All the gays say he's hot."

"I really shouldn't," I pled.

Fallon ignored me and drove into the parking garage to her reserved spot. Liam cradled his puppy, and we paraded into the building like we owned the place.

"I'm inviting the Conleys over," said Liam as the elevator sped up to the top floor. "My brother, Danny, texted. He's on his way."

The apartment, if you could call it that, was an entire house in the clouds. It had a large living room, a smaller dining room, a master bedroom, a guest room, and two baths. The living room was filled with modern furniture from wall to wall. There was a single picture—an enlarged black-and-white photograph of a bell pepper that appeared to have melted into the shape of a pair of lovers—hanging on the far wall. Photo books were placed about prominently but hadn't been opened by anyone from the looks of them.

Liam fretted over the pup. From an app, he ordered the delivery of a dog bed, ceramic bowls, toys, and an expensive brand of puppy food. While all of this was going on, Fallon removed a bottle of bourbon from the bar.

I've only been wasted a few times in my life. The third occasion was that evening, so I write with a good amount of caution about those events as they appear to me now like unrelated photographs floating in a puddle of rainwater. Fallon's legs were furled around Liam's waist. He was texting several people; then we ran out of cigarettes. Rather than order another delivery, I walked to the gas station on the corner. When I returned, Liam and Fallon were missing, so I cracked open one of those photo books—it may have been about famous skyscrapers—and pretended I was fascinated. Of course, the bourbon helped.

Already on my second drink, Fallon and Liam appeared in the living room, and guests were knocking at the apartment door—for how long, I didn't know; the bourbon was hitting me hard—it was Liam's brother, Danny. He was an earthy-looking hipster, near thirty, tan, his black hair falling under the straw fedora into his green eyes. He seemed to float through space, looking quite high but alert, like a bird of prey. He knew where everything was, so familiar was he with the place I asked him if he lived here.

"Do I live here?" repeated Danny. Then he laughed. "Dude, I live with a guy near campus."

The Conleys arrived next. Mr. Conley was too pale for a Texas summer. His face was smooth. He walked with a poise that set off my gaydar. He greeted everyone in the room, charming them with his manners. Then he turned his focus to me.

"I'm an artist. A photographer, to be specific. That picture is one of mine," he said, pointing to the ichorous pepper on the wall.

Mrs. Conley let out a shrill coo and gushed as she told me that her husband loved to photograph her breasts and vagina. I refilled my glass of bourbon.

Liam was now donning a pair of flamingo-colored chinos, a festive short-sleeved shirt with a beach motif, and white sneakers. His wardrobe change seemed to bring out a different side of his personality. Before, he was friendly. Now he interacted with affected conceit. As the minutes passed, and the more I drank, this change in him was more evident. He only laughed at his own jokes. He interrupted whoever was speaking to assert his opinion (whether he knew anything about the subject or not). In fact, the entire focus of the affair seemed to be about him.

"Danny," he began, nearly shouting. "Be careful around here. People are money-hungry, present company included. I hired a man last week to come here and give me a massage. Hot rocks, oils, and all. He offered a happy ending, and I said, 'Why not,' but I didn't realize he would charge me an extra hundred for it!"

"What was his name?" asked Mrs. Conley.

"Bruce, or something like that. But he prefers to only work on men."

"Hon, I so love your look today," said Mrs. Conley. "Those pants fit you quite well."

Liam wrinkled his nose and forehead at her.

"This schmatte? I just threw it together, and Fallon approved."

"But those pants," insisted Mrs. Conley. "They express so much." She was looking at his crotch. "That look needs to be documented. For posterity, you know. Brian needs to photograph you."

We all watched Liam adjust himself from right to left, leaving his hand between his legs. He grinned at us, enjoying our surprise and delight. Mr. Conley walked over to him and began making framing gestures with his fingers.

"I'd need more light," he said after taking a step back. "I want to focus on the edges of his face and contrast that with his lower regions. What kind of pose could—"

Mrs. Conley objected. "There's nothing wrong with the light, Brian."

"*Shh!*" said Mr. Conley. We all considered Liam again. Fallon made an exaggerated yawn and got up.

"Okay, Conleys, we all need you to have a drink," said Fallon. "Liam, get up and make them something before they bore us to death."

"There's no fucking ice. I told that damn delivery guy to bring ice." Liam had to compensate for being knocked down a level by Fallon. "Where do they find these people? None of them can follow instructions."

He leaned over the puppy, looked me in the eyes, and then drooled into its mouth. The dog lapped at his lips. "He really likes that, you know, Carry." He jumped to his feet and jogged to the kitchen as though he were in command of servants awaiting his next direction.

"I've shot some great photographs around Lake Travis," said Mr. Conley.

Fallon rolled her eyes.

"We have several framed downstairs."

"Several of what, Brian?"

"My work. One of my favorites I've entitled *Lake Travis—The Cliffs*."

"There are no cliffs around Lake Travis. There are small hills," said Fallon.

Danny sat down on the couch. His knee pressed against mine.

"Do you live here in Austin?" he asked.

"I'm out at Emerald Bluff."

"No shit! I was just over there at a party last month. It was at Jacobi's. Know him?"

"I'm his neighbor."

"He's a relative of Stefan Wertheimer. That's why he's so rich. At least that's what they say."

"No kidding."

He nodded.

"I love the parties, but I stay clear of the man. I would not want to get on his bad side."

I was transfixed with the information about Jacobi, and as I was letting it sink in, Mrs. Conley slapped her knee and gasped.

"Brian, you could create something wonderful with Danny! Or Liam and Danny, together," she said, holding out a finger on each hand in their direction. Mr. Conley touched his knuckle to the side of his lips and nodded. He tilted his head and turned toward Fallon.

"I'd like to photograph some of the celebrities who live at the lake if only I had a way in."

"Talk to Liam," said Fallon, laughing as he entered with cocktail glasses on a silver tray. "He'll introduce you to someone who rarely sits for a photograph, won't you, darling."

"Do what? Who?"

"You'll introduce Mr. Conley to your wife so he can photograph her." Her lips snarled, "S*hyla Kearns—At the Salon.*"

Danny draped his arm around my neck and whispered: "The only thing those two have in common is they both hate who they're married to."

"That can't be true."

"*Hate.* That's what they feel." He looked at Liam and then at Fallon. "Why don't they just fucking divorce their spouses? That's what I'd do. Then get married to each other the next day."

"But he must love Shyla on some level, don't you think?"

Liam had overheard my question, and his answer dazed me. "She's a goddamned cunt."

"Ha! See?" yelled Danny. "And as far as that one goes," he nodded at Fallon, "it's her husband who keeps her from getting what she wants. Catholics will go to hell if they divorce."

Donovan was not a Catholic, and I was confused why anyone would make up such a lie.

"But just wait and see," said Danny. "When they do get married, they'll move to Los Angeles and hide while things settle down."

"Wouldn't France be a better place to hole up?" I asked.

"France!" exclaimed Danny. "Have you been? I was just in Paris last year."

"Paris, eh?" I tried to sound interested.

"Yeah, me and this other guy I know went."

"How long were you there?"

"Long enough to waste ten thousand dollars. It was so boring. He wanted to see the art and architecture, and I wanted to eat and hit the bars. The whole thing was Les Miserable."

I didn't laugh at the joke but managed a smile. From the large window, I could see the Austin sky had turned pink and was tinged with gold. Maybe it was the surfeit of bourbon, but the colors were so vivid from this view. But Mrs. Conley's ear-piercing voice snapped me back inside.

"I had a near miss myself, darling," she said, already slurring a bit. "I nearly married a damn Jew. I loved how he chased after me, but really, he was low class. And everybody seemed to know it except me! They told me: 'Dierdre, drop him. He's trash.' If I hadn't have met Brian, I'd be baking challah bread and raising twelve children."

"Right!" said Liam, shaking his finger. "You *didn't* marry him."

"I'm aware of that."

"But I married her," said Liam. "And that's the pathetic difference between you and me."

"So, loser. Why did you?" asked Danny. "She didn't hold a gun to your head."

Liam chewed at his cheek and then sucked his teeth.

"I think I married her because I'd hoped she had more class than me. It turns out that puppy over there comes from better breeding."

"That's fucked up, bro. For a while, you were gaga over her. It was all, 'Shyla this and Shyla that.'"

"Everyone's like that in the beginning. But I was no crazier over her than I am about that guy sitting next to you."

When Liam pointed to me, everyone took an interest. I tucked in my chin and tried to look incredulous.

"The only crazy thing was actually marrying her. I knew it was a mistake when I found out she had to borrow her best friend's wedding dress. And she never said a word to me about it. The friend dropped by the salon to pick it up, but Shyla was out: 'Wait, that's *your* gown?' I said. 'I had no idea.' After she left with it, I punched a hole in the wall. Still there today."

Danny descended onto my ear again. "He needs to get away from her. I can't keep track of how long they've lived in that piece of shit motel. It should be condemned. Besides, Fallon is his first true love."

Another bottle of bourbon—was it the third or fourth?—traveled around the group except to Danny who "preferred weed over liquor." Fallon ordered pizzas, and we glutted, drinking more to keep the alcohol-to-food ratio steady enough to maintain the levity. I needed some air, but every time I got up to go for a walk around the pool, I was lassoed back to the sofa by strange yet important arguments that needed my attention. But a single thought persisted: What would the apartment look like to a stranger on the dark sidewalk next to this building? Maybe a man looks up, squints, and tries to imagine what is happening through the golden windows on the top floor. In my mind's eye, I see him, too, his curiosity, his confusion. I was in here and out there at the same time, spellbound and revolted by the importunity of consciousness and its endless varieties of expression.

Liam pulled up a chair close to me, and the heat from his body—or was it the bourbon?—carried his voice deep into my skin as he told me how he first met Fallon.

"It's always Friday nights when you can't find a rideshare service and taxis are too damn expensive. I'd been at my brother's and wanted to get downtown for a drink. So, I used this service called Ryde, knowing the car would be crammed with other people. I didn't care. But when the car came, it was empty. We stopped at the Domain, and she got in. She wore a white glittery dress, tight and low-cut around the tits but flowing and nearly see-through below her waist. She could have killed someone with the heels she was wearing. I couldn't stop staring at her. But when she gave me the side-eye, I pretended I was looking out her window at something interesting. We hit a bump on the way to the bar district, and she kicked me with those heels. I took out my phone and told her I was afraid for my life and pretended to dial 911. She laughed. And all I could think was life is too short; life is too damn short."

He looked at Mrs. Conley. Liam's fabricated laugh echoed around the living room.

"Dierdre, you can't stop staring at these pants, can you? I'll give them to you, unwashed, so you can sniff them whenever you want. And I'll buy an even better pair tomorrow. Anyway,

I have a shit-ton of things to do. Get a mani-pedi, a massage, a haircut; the puppy needs a nice collar with a name tag. Oh, wait, it needs a name, too! And I want one of those water shooting things for my teeth because I hate flossing."

"A Water Pik," I said.

"Yeah, one of those."

A minute ago, I looked at my watch, and it was nine. Now it's ten. Mr. Conley was passed out on a settee with his hands dangling loosely between his legs. His mouth was open. A bit of drool was considering making a run for it down his chin. He looked like one of the bog people of Ireland trapped beneath layers of peat. With my sleeve, I wiped the drool from his mouth; the indignity of it hanging there made me anxious.

The puppy was sitting on the floor trying to focus on Liam, but its eyes were glazed over from the ganja vapors. People strayed from the living room and then came back in, proposed to go here and there, and then forgot who they'd made plans with or lost the person entirely. It was around midnight when I heard Fallon and Liam yelling. I watched them stand nose to nose and jab their fingers at each other. I was afraid one of them would put a finger through the other's eye. They were fighting over Liam bringing up Donovan's name.

"Donovan. Donovan! DONOVAN!" screamed Liam. I can say it whenever I fucking want to! "Donovan! Dono—"

Fallon's hand cleaved the air and broke Liam's nose in one angry slice.

Then bloody towels piled up in the kitchen, and a chorus of admonishments sang out, and over all of this, a pathetic howl of pain. Mr. Conley was awake now. He stood and drifted toward the door. Nearly halfway there, he looked back at the spectacle—his wife and Danny yelling at Fallon, tripping over all the people bringing ice and more towels, and the lump of calamity still bleeding over the chair, the table, and the photo book of skyscrapers. Mr. Conley recommitted his feet toward the door. I followed him.

"Let's have lunch sometime," he said as we got off the elevator and stepped into the lobby.

"All right. Where?"

"Pick a place, and we'll go."

"You can't smoke in here, sir," yelled the doorman.

"What are you talking about?" snapped Mr. Conley.

"That cigar. At least fifteen feet away from the entrance."

"Oh, I'm so sorry. I wasn't aware I'd even been fingering it."

"Right. So, I'll pick a place," I continued.

…I stood next to his bed. He was naked, smoking that cigar sitting crossed-legged on top of a blue and paisley duvet. His endowment was palpable.

"Well, hon, what are you waiting for?"

Then I stretched and opened my eyes; light filtered into the room gently. I stared at the cup of coffee and the croissant resting on a tray next to Mr. Conley.

No Delphic sage is wanted to divine
The shape of Truth beneath my gauzy line;
Yet there are truths, like schoolmates, once well known,
But half remembered, not enough to own,
That, lost from sight in life's bewildering train,
May be, like strangers, introduced again,
Dressed in new feathers, as from time to time
May please our friends, the milliners of rhyme.

Astraea: The Balance of Illusions,
by Oliver Wendell Holmes

Chapter Three

Music boomed from Jacobi's house during the summer nights. People wandered in and out of his extravagant gardens like fireflies, wanting to see and to be seen among the decadent. In the afternoon, I watched his visitors diving off the top of his yacht or sunning on the rocks of his beach while jet skis cut the lake, sending foamy waves to the edge of the shore. His large Tesla became a party bus on the weekends, hauling people to and from Austin. This went on from early in the morning until long after midnight. On Mondays, his staff and landscapers worked all day to repair the pillage from the night before.

Every Friday, hundreds of platters of meats, cheeses, fruits, and kegs of beer arrived from Austin. And every Monday, the melted, gutted leftovers were stuffed into oversized garbage bags and loaded onto a truck. In the kitchen, there were juicers and espresso machines—enough for several butlers to operate—to keep the guests hydrated and caffeinated.

A squad of caterers set up tents in Jacobi's largest garden. They arranged flowers among the hors d'oeuvres, hams, pigs in a blanket, and golden-brown turkeys on white linen-covered buffet tables. Inside, the bar was stocked with top-shelf gin, scotch, bourbon, and liqueurs. They were so expensive that most young guests didn't know one from another, I suspected.

By seven o'clock, the band has arrived and set up, usually top-performing local artists. Sometimes a hip DJ visiting the city rocked the crowd. The last of the lake lovers found their legs and make their way to the dressing rooms upstairs; cars from all over Austin are parked five to ten deep in Jacobi's long driveway.

Suits and gowns paint the entertainment rooms, the balconies, and pool decks with colors that would make Van Gough blush. The bar is crowded, rounds of cocktails crowd surf to the garden until the atmosphere around Jacobi's mansion is charged with giddy laughter, and double entendres, and mawkish greetings between people who will never remember each other's names.

The myriad strands of white bulbs are more dazzling as the sun takes its leave in the west, and now the band is playing pink and purple funk music, and the crowd sings along at a feverish pitch. The more drinking, the more gaiety, emboldened by sybaritic delight and gushes at the slightest, happy greeting. There are no cliques; instead, people melt into one another the way sugar dissolves in water. New arrivals add to the mixture, and the solution becomes sweeter for it. Cocky young men and daring young women flirt with the regular guests (the line between genders has been erased already). They then gallop away victorious, off to the next verdant meadow offering more variety and attention, ever available under the display of dynamic lights.

One of these unfettered glories, glistening with glitter, grabs a martini from a tray, guzzles it down for good luck, and, moving her hands like Annie Morgan, ascends the dance platform alone. The crowd stops for a unified breath, entranced by her glorious maquillage; the band modulates the rhythm for her, and everyone erupts in applause as the rumor travels to every ear that this one is Natalie Mendoza's understudy from Moulin Rouge. The party has started.

On the first night I went to Jacobi's mansion, if memory serves, I was one of the few actually invited. Jacobi did not ask many people to come—the rest just showed up. They crammed themselves into Ubers which shuttled them out to Emerald Bluff, and by some mystery, they landed at Jacobi's door. Someone who knew him greeted the wild-eyed guests and, by implication, laid down the rules, much like the cast members at Disney World who welcomed the tourists at the ticket booths. Most came to these parties and left without so much as seeing Jacobi. They came to carouse, to seduce, to dream, and that was their ticket to gain entrance.

As I said, I had been invited. A young man in an absurd white uniform cut across my yard early that Saturday morning with a hand-written note from his boss: *I would be exceedingly pleased*, it said, *if you came to my little shindig tonight. I've noticed you many times and wanted to invite you over, but something always got in the way of a proper invitation*—it was signed Oskar Jacobi, with perfect penmanship.

Bedecked in a tan, checkered sport coat with a mustard-colored handkerchief tucked in the front pocket, a white shirt, navy pants, and loafers (no socks, of course), I walked over to his garden shortly after seven and wandered the seemingly endless spaces filled with bodies, food, and drink. I was uncomfortable not knowing anyone. I was taken in by all the college men scattered about, all of them too handsome and too groomed, eager to talk to anyone they pegged as a regular. They were hungrily attentive to the quick and easy current of money and perhaps thought they might snag some for themselves if they sang the right tune.

I moved on to the house to find Jacobi, but the few people I had the courage to stop and ask about him looked at me as though I'd just assaulted them and made it clear that no one knew where he was and that he was rarely ever seen. I slithered away to the cocktail bar in the garden where, standing all alone with a drink in my hand, I hoped not to look creepy.

I progressed from tipsy to sloshed in minutes, swallowing my embarrassment in one sip after another, when Levi Safran appeared on the steps, leaning against a pillar and surveying the garden. And me.

I staggered toward him, not caring if he were interested in company or not. I needed someone I knew to undo my feelings of inadequacy before returning the friendly greetings of the other guests.

"Well, hi," I thundered, walking toward him, certain I spoke too loudly as heads turned in my direction.

"You're here," he said. "That figures, of course, given you live next to—"

He took my hand, as warm and welcoming as a mannequin's, although the gesture reassured me nonetheless that he would be there for me as soon as he handled the two people standing at the bottom of the stairs. I couldn't tell if they were men or women. They dressed alike, but their silver clothing and neon hairstyles offered no hint of their gender. And I didn't care at that moment. They were both attractive.

"Hey, Levi," they said in unison. "It's tragic you didn't win, darling."

They were talking about Krav Maga. Levi had lost the match last week.

"You don't remember us," one of them said, "but we met you at a party here last month."

"You've changed your hair since then, honey," said Levi, and my face felt like it had grown twice its size and no longer fit my head. "You look so fish." But the neon-haired people in silver vanished, and his observation was caught only by the empty space in front of us. Levi put his muscular, golden-brown arm in mine, and we floated down the steps and paraded ourselves about the garden. Cocktails, like meteors, shot through the starlit sky, and we sat down at a table with the silver people and three guys. Each of them slurred their names, so I only remember them sounding like a string of vowels, scant with consonants.

"Are you here every weekend?" Levi asked of the silver person beside him.

"Not yet. This is our second time," they said in an assertive tone. They turned to their twin: "Same with you, Lux?"

It was the same for Lux.

"It's nice here," Lux said. "But I don't give a fuck what I'm doing or where, as long as it's fun. Last time I tore my Wildfang jumpsuit on the dance platform, and Jacobi asked for my name and address—in a few days, a package from Nordstrom arrived with a new jumpsuit in it."

"Did you like it?" asked Levi.

"Hell yeah! I have a friend who can sew, and they're going to tighten up the chest for me. It's watermelon-red with bronze buttons and a silver chain. One hundred and seventy-five dollars."

"There's something weird about a guy who would do something like that," said the other silver person. "He must let stuff go to his head. He probably doesn't want anybody having something on him."

"Who?" I asked.

"Jacobi. Somebody told me—"

The silver neon-haired pair and Levi leaned in to conspire.

"I heard he's a murderer."

Titillation zapped through us like a current. The three drunk guys careened their heads toward us, curious now.

"I don't think he killed anyone," said Lux. "I think he's a spy."

One of the guys nodded in agreement.

"I overheard the exact thing from an Israeli who knew all about him," he confided.

"Nah," said the first silver person, "he couldn't be a spy because he's too wrapped up in his businesses and US politics." We were back in their corner now and were eager to hear more. "Watch him when he thinks no one is looking. He's got the expression of a killer."

They concentrated their eyes on us and shuddered. Lux shuddered. Together we searched for Jacobi. It didn't occur to me at the time, but this was precisely the kind of speculation Jacobi wanted; the rumors fueled his image and sparked the imaginations of people who had little else going on in their lives.

First supper—the second would be served after midnight—was being offered, and Levi asked me to join his group, which was gathered around a table on the other side of the garden. Present were three couples and Levi's date, an overachieving UT student, brash, and confident that he was going to get into Levi's pants. Levi's entourage maintained a noble air, intending to portray the superiority of The Hollows over Emerald Bluff, and made sure to safeguard the optics at all times, not wanting to appear to have joined the revelry of the rest.

"Carry, let's leave," whispered Levi, after an unseemly hour and a half of foolish posturing; "I'm over all of this."

He told the group we were going to find Jacobi. "Carry has never met him, which is giving him some anxiety."

The UT boy nodded and waved us off, looking forlorn. We searched the bar first. It was crowded, but no Jacobi. He wasn't at the top of the steps, and we couldn't find him on any of the balconies. Levi snapped his fingers and took my hand. A majestic-looking door, made of solid wood and stained glass, opened on an oak-paneled library. It looked like a grand room from the Titanic, restored. A slender man, in his fifties, with a crooked nose and piercing dark eyes, was perched like a raven, obviously drunk, on the edge of an elaborate oval-shaped desk. He was surveying the shelves of books with bizarre concentration. The man whipped his head toward us and inspected Levi when we came in.

"Tell me your opinion," he said.

"Opinion about what?"

He stretched out his hand and spread his fingers, waving them across the bookshelves.

"All of this. Never mind," he sighed. "I don't need your opinion. I can already tell."

"Tell what?"

"They're genuine."

"You're talking about the books, hon?" asked Levi.

"What else? They're legitimate—including the pages. I thought they might be props, but they are the genuine article. Take a look."

Assuming we were skeptical about the books, the man dashed to the bookcases and selected *Letters to a Young Poet* by Rilke.

"Observe!" he said as he flipped the pages of the book. "I told you these were real. I was shocked. This man has outdone Lamont, but Jacobi knew where to stop, unlike him. Nothing overboard, you see. But what would you expect from a man like Jacobi? And who invited you?" he asked. "Or did you just show up like the others? I was invited. Some of us were invited."

Levi considered the raven-eyed man with a benevolent face without answering.

"I was invited by a woman named Grace Richards," he said. "Know of her? We met somewhere last night. I can't remember where exactly. I've been drunk out of my mind the whole week, and I hoped sitting in this room would sober me up."

"Are you sober now?"

"A drop soberer, I think. I've only been here an hour, so I can't tell. Will you look at these books, people! They're legitimate. Absolutely—"

"Yes, we've been over that."

We offered a pitiful wave and hurried back outside.

The dancing platform was teeming with people; older men were grinding against young women, elite couples clung to each other in the uncongested corners—and a throng of boys and girls danced by themselves. By midnight, the buffoonery had multiplied. A DJ gave the band a break, spinning white-hot sounds while a cluster of people did flips, tossed a ham back and forth to each other, and a girl tried to juggle three candles without extinguishing the flames. Raucous laughter exploded toward the summer sky, as though it were being offered up like incense to the gods. The silver neon-haired people jumped onto the stage in costumes. They were dressed as furries, one a rabbit and the other a dog. Their act included a terrible chase, and then an actual fight, ending with the dog screwing the rabbit. Apparently, the rabbit protested at first, and then hungrily yielded to desire for the hypersexualized dog. The champagne was served in beer steins now, and the moon watched over this bacchanal, rising higher every hour to gain a better view, casting her light upon the lake, tiny floating diamonds shimmering in time with the beat.

I was sitting with Levi at a table. There was a man a little older than me and a boisterous young girl. She laughed before the end of any joke and squealed when the man tickled the air with his fingers. I was having a blast. I had downed two steins of champagne, and the ambiance had transformed into something primordial and metaphysical.

The man squeezed my hand and smiled.

"You look familiar," he said. "Where do you work?"

"I was hired on at Greater Together."

"That's it! I knew I'd seen you before."

We talked a few moments about the social campaigns I was directing. He lived on the lake and told me he'd just bought a new boat and would be testing it out in the morning.

"Would you like to join me, mate?"

"What time?"

"Whenever you're free, my friend."

I was just about to ask his name when Levi squeezed my arm and smiled.

"Having a good time now?" he asked.

"It's fabulous." I turned to my new friend.

"This is an eccentric party, if I'm honest. And the strangest part is I haven't even seen the host! I live just over there." I pointed at the darkened cottage nearly concealed by the hedge. "And this guy, Jacobi, sent over one of his staff with a handwritten invitation."

He blinked and looked at me as if I were a math problem to solve.

"I'm Jacobi," he blurted out.

"What? I'm so sorry."

"I thought you knew who I was, mate. I guess that makes me a lousy host."

He smiled at me as if there were nothing to forgive. But more than that, it was a smile that had a way of making you feel like you'd be safe forever, as long as he was the one smiling at you. His smile projected that security like a lighthouse and then centered that light on *you* promising an inevitable bias in your favor. His smile accepted you as much as you wanted to be accepted, it had faith in you in the way you would like to have faith in yourself, and somehow it guaranteed that it had already witnessed the best of who you were. I was utterly softened. As soon as I was aware of an aching desire for him, his smile disappeared—and I saw a dignified ruffian, a few years over thirty, whose ornate speech and mannerisms were just short of irrational. Before he had introduced himself, I had a notion that he was choosing his words with unnatural forethought.

A butler ran up to Mr. Jacobi. Breathless, he informed him that "the call" had come in from New York. The butler gave each of us a slight nod and then ran back to the house.

"If there's anything you need, mate, anything at all, just let one of my staff know," he said to me. "I apologize for the interruption. I'll find you later."

After he left, I touched Levi's shoulder—compelled to show him my interest. I had imagined Jacobi a fat, lobster-like old man.

"Who is he?" I asked him. "What do you know about him?"

"He's none other than Jacobi, darling. Just a man."

"Where did he grow up? What does he do?"

"Now *you've* been infected," he said with a forced smile. "He's fond of saying he went to Harvard."

A blurry image in my mind began to form, but his follow-up comment threw it even more out of focus.

"But I'm sure he's lying."

"What makes you so sure?"

"He doesn't seem like the Harvard type."

The way Levi said it reminded me of the silver person's outburst that they had heard Jacobi was a murderer and only goaded my curiosity. If the answer had been that Jacobi grew up in Pittsburgh or Cleveland, I would have easily believed it. I could conceive of a history like that. But men in their thirties didn't—at least in my limited experience of the world—materialize out of thin air and build a mansion on Emerald Bluff.

"But all this is beside the point. He throws these large soirees that border on orgies," said Levi, dodging my questions with a metropolitan taste for the abstract. "And I do love them so. I find they're more personal. You just can't have any privacy over cocktails with a few people."

There was a horrible screech from the microphone, and the DJ's voice cut through the blather of the garden.

"Party people," he yelled. "Mr. Jacobi has asked the band to play Cream Boys' latest single. It's all over the charts, and if you follow them on social media, you know they're gonna go big." He cupped his hand to his ear, inspiring deafening cheers, whooping, and applause. "The song is called," his voice full of libido, "'Shake My Money Tree!'"

I'd never heard the song and wasn't following it because, after the intro, I saw Jacobi standing by himself on the steps watching the crowd with pleasure in his eyes. His olive skin was smooth and his golden-brown hair was cut short on the sides but left wavy on top, perfectly combed. I searched for something corrupt in him. Perhaps the fact that he wasn't drunk set him apart from the rest of us, for he was the only one who appeared clean and vivid. His bright aura grew as the revelry increased. When "Shake My Money Tree" was over, the DJ played a long set of electronic chill-out house. Gender and age evaporated—girls swayed with girls, boys embraced boys, men and women caressed in a slow vibration of ecstasy. But no one looked at Jacobi, no boy nor girl reached for his hand, no suitors approached him for a dance. He had a way of being lonely in a space, or just by being in that space making it lonely.

"Excuse me, sir."

Jacobi's butler was standing beside us all at once.

"Mr. Safran," he said, "would you mind coming with me? Mr. Jacobi wants to see you. Alone."

"Me?" he gasped.

"Yes, sir."

He rose out of his chair as if in slow motion, glancing at me with surprise and confusion, and walked behind the butler toward the mansion. As I watched him, it occurred to me that his tuxedo, in fact, all of his clothes, hung on him too squarely, as if they had been tailored for someone else.

I was alone now at the table, and it was nearly two. The breeze carried down bewitching sounds from an open window that hung over the veranda. Levi's UT undergrad spoke with two animated boys and invited me to join them. I went inside.

The large hall was crowded with bodies. One of the silver neon-haired people was beating on a drum set and towering over them was a pink-haired famous rapper engaged in the beat. They had drunk copious amounts of champagne, and during their performance, having misread the room, decided what everyone needed to hear were some rhymes about the plight of animals soon to be extinct. They wailed in the spaces between lyrics and then picked up the next line in a shaky, hoarse voice. Anger disfigured their face, appearing to crack their thick, dry makeup. Someone yelled out that they should get a clue, and they threw down the mic, collapsed into a chair, and fell asleep.

"Their partner killed their cat last week," explained a girl at my right.

Arguments broke out among couples. Levi's entourage from The Hollows had broken up due to a vicious disagreement. One of the men was feeling up a young local news anchor, and his wife tried to break them up with a flirtatious gesture. She snapped and employed sharper weapons when that failed: insults and guilt. She stormed off to get another cocktail and then returned like a stoked fire and screamed: "You bastard. You said you wouldn't do this again."

Bitter husbands and wives weren't the only ones exchanging heated discussions about leaving. Two conceited sober guys stood over their dates, both glorious drag queens, who were bellyaching in defiant sisterhood.

"At the first smell of fun in the water, this one wants to go home."

"Gurl, you need to bring someone with more stamina next time."

"We're usually gone by now, darling."

"Us, too."

"Not tonight!" huffed one of the men. "The band left thirty minutes ago."

The queens protested, and heads turned. Finally, both men grabbed their girl by the arm and dragged them out, screaming and spitting.

I was alone again in the hall. The library door opened, and Levi and Jacobi walked out together. He whispered one last thing into Levi's ear, but his ambitious face dropped, replaced by decorum as people fought past each other to tell him goodbye.

Levi's splintered group motioned from the porch and begged him to leave, but he stayed to shake hands.

"Baby, Jacobi just spilled the tea," he whispered to me.

"You were with him in there for almost an hour."

"What I heard will rock your world amazing," he said. "But he made me promise not to tell."

"Then why torture me with something you can't tell me?"

His large mouth yawned in my face. "Come visit me, darling. Get my number from Fallon." He scampered away, still speaking—his small brown fingers flittered at me in the air.

Now I was stuck. Nearly everyone had left except for a few of Jacobi's guests who were flanking him. I decided to join.

"Mr. Jacobi, I want you to know that I looked for you all night. I'm sorry I didn't recognize you in the garden earlier."

"Don't be ridiculous," he encouraged me. "That's behind us now, mate." His hand came to rest on my shoulder. "Just be ready at the boat tomorrow morning, nine o'clock sharp."

Again, the butler approached Mr. Jacobi, already prepared with an apologia.

"London is calling, sir."

"Tell them I'm coming to the phone."

"Good night."

"Good night." He smiled—and I felt there must be some meaning in being the last to leave as if that was his plan all along. "Good night, mate."

As I walked down the steps, I saw the final shebang of the whole affair. Headlights pierced the darkness in a ditch beside the road not far from the mansion. Figures walked about the scene like apparitions. A new Porsche which had just left Jacobi's minutes ago was sitting upright in the ditch, one of its wheels still gyrating on the pavement. Cars and people blocked the exit, and the drivers who lined up behind them were in an uproar.

A thin man standing in the middle of the road eyed the car and the tire, and then people gathered around to help him.

"You see," he said. "The car went into the ditch. That is a fact."

I first recognized his sense of awe, and then the man himself—it was raven-eyes from the library.

"How did you manage this?"

"I have no idea," said the man, hands shaking in the air. "I'm not a professional car driver."

"Did you hit a wall or something?"

"I wouldn't be the one to ask," said the man, his eyelids fluttering. "I don't drive often. Hardly ever. I just found myself here, nothing else to say."

"If you don't drive very often, what the hell are you doing behind the wheel of a Porsche?"

"Well, that's my car. Who can say?"

Everyone was quiet now.

"Were you trying to kill yourself, dude?"

"At least it was just a tire. For a man who doesn't drive very often, it could have been way worse."

"I think you have missed my point," said raven-eyes. "I wasn't the one driving. He was," and he pointed to the door of the Porsche, now open, where someone let out a groan from inside. The crowd—it was a mob by now—gulped and stepped back. Then one foot made contact with the ground, and then the other. The man stood, knees shaking, and held onto the dangling door.

Blinded by the headlights and frightened from the blaring car horns, the ghost took a step toward raven-eyes.

"What the hell?" he asked, dazed. "Did somebody hit us?"

A wave of fingers pointed at the dusty tire in the road. He considered it and then looked into the bushes as if he thought it might have rolled out from the brush.

"No, idiot," someone said. "You did that."

He wrinkled his face in disbelief.

"I didn't even know we'd stopped."

He stamped his feet. Then he closed his eyes as if in meditation and inhaled deeply. He stood erect, forcing his shoulders back, and asked, "Would someone be so kind as to tell me where the nearest gas station is?"

A few men, a little soberer than he was, tried to explain that the wheel was no longer attached to the car.

"I'll just back it out."

"The goddamn tire is off, bro!"

He looked at the tire.

"Might as well give it a try."

The cacophony of horns had given me a headache. I left them all there and walked across the yard to my cottage. Like Lot's wife, I couldn't resist taking one last look back at them. The moon was now a lonely, radiant disc paused over Jacobi's house restoring stillness to the night, the only guest lingering in his empty garden. The windows and doors exhaled with exhaustion, framing the lone Jacobi, who stood on the porch, his hand raised in a polite farewell.

* * *

Jacobi's yacht, a million-dollar Atlas X-series, was a motionless iceberg on the lake. Its four levels housed sixteen beds, five bathrooms, two kitchens, a hot tub, and a helipad.

Jacobi greeted me with a firm handshake. And with that accepting smile.

"Did you notice her name?" he asked, nodding at the ship.

"No, what is it?"

"Oskarholic's Anonymous."

"Fitting," I said.

We boarded the yacht and took the stairs to one of the helms. There were more consoles, displays, and buttons on that ship than on some airplanes I had flown in.

"I'll take her out of the berth, and we'll follow the Colorado toward Muleshoe Bend. Then you can take over."

I broke out in a cold sweat, and my mouth went dry. "I'm barely comfortable being on a boat, Mr. Jacobi. I don't want to steer one."

He laughed so hard he had to palm my shoulder for balance. "I'm only kidding, mate. After we get our bearings, we'll take breakfast downstairs. You are hungry, aren't you?"

"Famished," I lied.

We moved at such a fast clip or so it seemed—I'm no expert—that navigating stairs and furniture was a hazard. Along the bow, I jostled into Jacobi such that he had to hold my arm until we sat down at a table.

"If I'd known this would be such an ordeal for you, I would have suggested we do something else, mate."

"I'll be fine. Not much boating going on in Oberlin," I said.

"Your hometown?"

"Home, yes. But maybe it's more like a village than a town."

"I prefer places I can get lost in," he said.

"And yet hundreds of people visit your home every weekend."

"Exactly. I like people the way I like a boat. I can get on and off when I want, and I always take note of where the lifeboats are."

"That must be lonely for you." I remembered him standing on those marble steps last night, unaccompanied, surveying his guests like a farouche adolescent on the first day of school.

"At the end of the day, we're all alone."

"We don't have to be—"

"You're an attractive man, Carry Iverson. Now that you're in Austin, maybe romance is in your future."

He covered my hand with his. I would come to understand that these free and easy touches were a presupposition of friendship. At times they seemed fatuous, but there on the boat, calculated, as though Jacobi were preparing me for a voyage into his soul, which was something I craved from him except I yearned to receive it by his lips, his taste, his skin that smelled clean, as though scented with bergamot and vetiver.

I had possessed this ineluctable desire all my life—and now it was staring me in the face.

I suddenly felt sick. I pushed myself out of the chair and made for the starboard railing. As I clung to it, heaving, Jacobi wiped my mouth with a damp napkin.

"Let's go downstairs to the living quarters. I have Dramamine and a comfortable bed."

The large room was like a master suite from a hotel. The burgundy and white tiles on the floor softly reflected golden inset lighting on the ceiling. Marblewood cabinets and dressers lined the walls and made an open space in the center of the room for the bed. I fell onto the soft linen sheets. Jacobi took off my shoes. Whatever was happening between us reflected in the mirror above. I held my gaze there because I couldn't bear to see his sympathy directly.

Jacobi pulled up a chair close to me and sat down.

"You said you moved to Austin for work," he said, dabbing my forehead with a cool cloth. "Was that the only reason?"

"My cousin is here. The family back in Ohio wouldn't have supported the move otherwise."

"Is their approval so important to you?"

"In some ways," I said.

"There's nothing like a fresh start to help you discover what kind of man you are, mate."

"Is that why you came to Austin?" I asked.

Jacobi's face became hard as if he were trying to conceal something painful. Or perhaps he became uncomfortable with our propinquity. He cleared his throat. "Where does your cousin live?"

"The Hollows," I said.

Jacobi leaned back in his chair. "The Hollows," he repeated under his breath.

Outside, the winds died down and the susurration of the lake encouraged me to return topside. Back at the table, Jacobi was restive, his every word measured and his gestures revealed too much. His gaze hopped from lake to hill to me in a restless circuit.

"Now may not be the best time to bring this up, but I'm curious." The curiosity blossomed in his face, and then wilted into a doleful scintilla of fear. Its withered petals cascaded down his shirt to crackle away into his hands. "There might be a bit of a family issue between us. We need to address it."

He wanted to tell me something. It was there on the tip of his tongue, or in the lake that whirled in his mind, but the words sunk like wreckage, unsalvageable for the moment, and thus remained his and his alone; only Jacobi knew what distressed him. Distressed and stirred him so that they became the same, a singular apprehension.

***

As I read over what I've written so far, I feel as though I may have misled the reader into thinking that what happened on three nights, spread out weeks apart, were the only things going for me. The truth is, they were low-key events on my busy summer calendar. And at some later point, they preoccupied me much less than what was going on in my personal life.

My workload increased, and I was directing even more social campaigns. I woke before the sun peaked over the hills around the lake to avoid the rush-hour traffic into Austin. I'd become buddies with my coworkers and rotated lunches with my favorites in crowded, bright downtown eateries. I even shacked up a few times with a boy who lived in West Lake Hills, but in July, when he left to vacation in Spain, the broil had slowed to a simmer.

I usually ate dinner at The Upside—it was the most depressing time of day—and then I returned to the office for a dedicated hour to research potential targets like certain politicians, CEOs, and celebrities. After that, I walked down Sixth Street, turning south at Colorado, and stopped at a couple of bars on Fourth.

Austin was growing on me, the unfussy, risk-taking atmosphere at night, and the pleasure the parade of such a variety of men gave to the hungry eye. After a few drinks, I liked to continue down Fourth and discover hot guys in the crowd and fantasize that soon I would be a part of their lives, and there would be no one here to judge me. When the mood struck, I even followed some of them to their apartments. Sometimes, one would reach his door, turn to me, and invite me in. Then there were the times when the bruised purple-blue sky over Austin brought on nagging loneliness that I sensed in others too—the young workforce hanging out in front of bars until it was time for them to go home alone—young men in the dark witnessing the keenest moments of life slipping past them.

When the streets leading into the bar district were lined with pulsating cars, I felt my heart drop into my stomach. Shadows of bodies mingled inside, people shouted greetings to one another, and laughter rang out. Party colors glowed from vape pens in dizzying circles. In my mind, I pretended that I, too, was in a hurry to catch some thrill and would soon share in their adventure. Yet I was certain that I was the most unhappy person on the street and the loneliest because none of these people knew what was crushing me inside.

But what if we are all trees in a decaying forest trying to revive our riven, storm-tossed branches snapping from the wind until dejection shears them off completely? And one can hear thud after thud of our decomposed limbs battering the ground, and even so, we smile and walk proudly around town, for we're all hoping for some kind soul to transplant us from our blighted and scorched lives and say, "You belong here, friend."

Levi and I didn't see each other for some time, and then we reconnected in the middle of summer. At first, I considered his company a boost to my image because he knew whoever should be known, and they knew him. And he was hot. Then my feelings toward him changed. I didn't love him, per se, but I was intrigued. The cavalier attitude he held out to the world masked something with more depth—this is what most masks do until they can no longer—and one day, I saw through a gaping crack in his.

We were at a party in West Austin, and he'd left the top to his rented convertible down during a downpour and then lied about it. And the backstory I'd missed that night at Donovan's eventually got around to me. The championship he "almost" won wasn't entirely accurate. He *had* won it, but the Israeli panel of judges disqualified him. They accused Levi of lying about his gender. The thing blew into a scandal in the Krav Maga world and between right-wingers and LGBTQ advocates in America. While I could understand it was not anyone's business what gender he was, I noticed a pattern of deception.

Levi Safran's knee-jerk reaction was to avoid perceptive people because he assumed he was safer among those who couldn't detect deviations from the norm. But this coping mechanism had spun wildly out of his control and now he was fatally deceitful. He had not been taught how to push through prejudice and adversity and I imagine he employed sophistry at an early age to keep that cold, contemptuous face turned to the world and still satiate the needs of his vivacious body.

But I didn't care. If a person has to lie because the body they were born with doesn't feel natural, I could place no blame—I felt sorry for him, and then I forgot about it. It was on the way to the same party that we argued about driving. He came so close to clipping a car the other driver had to swerve as he passed.

"Do you actually have a driver's license?" I asked. "You should be more careful."

"You think I'm not a good driver?"

"You're a terrible driver."

"It's not me, darling; it's the assholes around me."

"That has nothing to do with how you handle a car," I said.

"It does because if I drive offensively, they'll stay out of my way."

"And what if you come across another offensive driver?"

"I don't think about it. I don't like offensive people," he said. "That's why I like you."

His white sunglasses shielded his gray, wolflike eyes, which now observed the road more carefully. But he had turned the topic to our relationship on purpose, and I think I felt something like love. But I am methodical and thrive on my own rules, which often tether my passion to the shore. Before I could explore anything with Levi, I needed to detach myself from the debacle in Ohio. I'd been emailing every day and closing with: "Love, Carry," and all I could think of was that sweet boy as he played the piano, his slender fingers touching the keys the same way he glided his hands over my neck. We both knew it was over, but the rope had to be cut as gently as possible before I could move on.

Plato said there were four virtues, and everyone hopes they have at least one, and this is mine: I am the most cautious person I know.

We make ourselves a place apart
Behind light words that tease and flout,
But oh, the agitated heart
Till someone find us really out.
'Tis pity if the case require
(Or so we say) that in the end
We speak the literal to inspire
The understanding of a friend.
But so with all, from babes that play
At hide-and-seek to God afar,
So all who hide too well away
Must speak and tell us where they are.

"Revelation" by Robert Frost

Chapter Four

On Sunday morning, while the halyards slapped against the masts, the elite of Emerald Bluff and The Hollows returned to Jacobi's mansion and graced his lawn.

"He's a drug dealer," said a young woman circulating between his liquor and his flowers. "He killed a man who had discovered that he was a direct descendant of Hitler."

"Pick me that orchid, darling, and pour me another mimosa," said another, loafing on one of his loungers. "If you strip away the wealthy exterior, you don't see a drug dealer. But I did hear that one of his businesses is a front for prostitution."

"Both of you are wrong," interjected an older man with an outdated mustache and suit. "You're right, of course; he's not what he appears to be. And that is because he's a gutless fool. He cooked up some excuse to get discharged from the army in Afghanistan."

"Maybe he has an oil scheme going with the Arabs," said the woman, now sipping the mimosa.

Once, I made a spreadsheet of the names of the guests who came to Jacobi's mansion that summer. I titled it "A Record of Jacobi's Guests Beginning July 5th, 2021." The list will give you a better illustration than my memory of who consumed Jacobi's graciousness and returned his kindness by not caring to know anything about him.

From The Hollows came the Sorensons and the Chavezs, and a man named Chamberlain, whom I knew from Oberlin, and Elizabeth Crews who drowned recently in Lake Travis. And the Fauberts and the Shadids, and an entire family named

Fiorentino who always gravitated to one corner and snubbed other guests. And the Zimmermans and the Tokaryevs (or rather Estevan Ribeiro and Mrs. Tokaryev's husband), and Adnan Göransson who woke up one winter morning, as the rumor goes, with white streaks in his full head of black hair.

Brad Morris was from The Hollows, if my list is correct. He only attended one party in a blue tuxedo and had a fistfight with one of the staff in the garden. From Marble Falls came the Barneses and the Ephraimsons and Frank and Annie Moles of Arkansas, and Lungs and George and Elli Wallis. Mr. Wallis had to crash at Jacobi's for several days before he was carted off to jail. He was so smashed out of his mind and laid out on the driveway that Mrs. Blanchard's Uber ran over his leg. The Michels came once or twice, and Leroy L. Ruggles who was nearly eighty, and Asta Vestergaard, and the Tsukamotos, and Baba, the curator of fine rugs, and her girls.

From Emerald Bluff came the Simonds and the Giles and Cheryl Russell and Carlisle the congressman and Joe Bostwick who owned Metropolitan Films, and Stephanie and Angela Adler and Burt Bensoussan Sr. and Daniel (Jr.) and Angus Martin, all involved with filmmaking in some way. And the Gonclaves and the Krugers and Jasmine Stevenson, sister to the same Stevenson who later poisoned her lover. Manfrin, the attorney, came often, and Isabel Collum and John "The Badger" Conway and the Fús and Donna Slaughter—all came to gamble—and when Conway left for a drink in the garden, it meant he was out, and Badger Construction would take a dip in profits the next day.

A man named Pfeffer showed up so often that he was given the nickname "the roommate"—none of us thought he had a place of his own. Many actors came like Bertram Gilkey and Annalis Niesen and James Bolling and Michael Frase and Sharon Mcleod. From Chicago were The Radcliffes and the Soderbergs and the Ayalas and Paul Knight and the Hixsons and the

LaGrandes and the Thorps and the young Webers, divorced, and Anthony Walls who committed suicide by jumping from the John Hancock Center on Michigan Avenue.

Jim McWhorter always came with three or more women. They were always different but only in form; they were so alike that I always assumed they had been there before.

I also remember George Bottoms came once and the Mullis boys and young Ruben who had his jaw blown off in a convenience store robbery, and Mr. Ackerman and Mr. Dresner, his fiancée, and Lara Pereira Pinto and Mr. Delaney, a former priest, and Miss Evelyn Cao with a woman she told everyone was her live-in maid, and some low-ranking member of the Royal Family (whom we called Princess), but I've forgotten his real name.

All of these came to Jacobi's mansion that summer.

***

Late in July, at nine o'clock one morning, Jacobi's Bentley Bacalar pulled up in the driveway to my cottage. He tapped the horn twice and turned up his stereo. This was the first time he had visited my place, even though I had attended two of his parties, had gone for a ride on his boat, and, by his request, often swam at his beach.

"Good morning, mate. We're having lunch together, so we might as well go in my car."

He was balanced on the hood of the Bacalar with such poise, so feline, yet childlike. This spontaneous energy always seemed to push through his ceremonious facade when we were together. He was terminally fidgeting, his manicured fingernails tapping on something, cracking his knuckles, and sometimes, he touched me on the back of my forearm. It was more than a touch, at least I thought so at the time. His beautiful hands squeezed my muscles and lingered a few seconds too long to consider it a friendly gesture.

He noticed I was lusting after his car.

"He's a handsome one, isn't he, mate?" He slid off so I could take it all in. "You haven't seen it before?"

Of course, I had seen it. Who hadn't? It was metallic flame-yellow, stout in the front with its grill and bespoke front lights, stocky vents, and diffuser, but sleek and muscular toward the rear with carbon-fiber wings. Inside it was outfitted in Riverwood trim and moose-skin upholstery.

Jacobi and I spoke at least a dozen times in the past month, and I wondered if I had made some blunder as he had very little to say. But then it occurred to me that perhaps he had been betrayed by so many people he was simply reserved.

And then we took that terrifying drive into Austin. We weren't a few miles away from Emerald Bluff when Jacobi became playful, flirty, and effusive.

"Don't hold back on me, mate," he started. "What's your opinion of me?"

My mind was awash with options about how to answer his question, so I pitched some evasive generalizations. "You have everything going for you. I admire that," I said.

"And?"

"And I could learn so much from you. I hope—"

"You're not going to go for it, are you. Then I'll tell you some things about me," he said, stopping me mid-sentence. "I'm sure you've heard all the rumors, the current ones anyway, and I don't want you to base your perception of me on those absurd stories. May God strike me down if I'm lying." He raised his hand as if to take a vow. "I'm the son of affluent people in the Midwest—may they rest in peace. I attended Harvard, just like all the men in my family before me. It's our tradition, you see."

He glanced at me sideways—this is why Levi said he was lying. He tripped over phrases like "attended Harvard," as though he were trying to get out something dodgy. My confidence in his autobiography fractured, like safety glass after a wreck.

"Where in the Midwest?" I asked.

"Minneapolis."

"Great city. I've visited a few times. But the cost of living there is high."

"I inherited all of my family's wealth."

His voice was sedated as if he were still in shock over the decimation of his clan. The thought that he was trying to pull one over on me kept nagging at my gut. But his face became so still and expressionless that I gave him the benefit of the doubt.

"Then I traveled to the big cities in Europe and the Middle East. I lived like a baron. I collected art, antique coins, furniture, anything to take my mind off a past wound."

He was so dramatic. And corny. I wasn't sure whether to console him or laugh but the image of him dressed like Lawrence of Arabia trekking across the desert provided me no direction.

"Then I moved on to riskier things. I had a death wish. I climbed La Rage D'Adam outside of Monaco. I went paragliding over Ölüdeniz, Turkey. Kayaked down Rainbow Falls on the Wailuku River—it was an eighty-foot drop." He paused to let that sink in. Then: "I even BASE jumped twenty-one thousand feet off Meru Peak in the Himalayas. I still hold the record!" he said with a smile. But it was a thin smile, pressed, blanched, as one who greets his opponent who has just beaten him. That raw smile was a badge of resignation, worn by a man well-acquainted with trouble.

My disbelief had changed into an infatuation for him. I couldn't hear enough. What he had given me was like a minuscule sample from a few portions of an extensive buffet. As if he heard my thoughts, he pulled a photograph out of his pocket.

"I bring this with me wherever I go, mate. It was taken back in the day at Harvard Square. The man with me is now one of the nine on the Supreme Court."

I took the photograph from him. Two men in sweaters and jeans leaned on each other outside Cafe Algiers. A younger Jacobi was nibbling an ear lobe of the other man.

Suddenly, all of his stories were true. Jacobi of Arabia horseback riding in Morocco. Extreme Sport Jacobi falling thousands of feet through the air. Harvard educated Jacobi now surrounded by his collection of things that chip away at his broken soul.

"I'm going to ask a favor of you today," he said, sliding the photo into his pocket, "so you needed to know more about me. I had to dispel the rumors so you wouldn't think I was a charlatan." He hesitated and then said, "I keep the company of strangers because letting people too close only ends in misery. I'll ask you about this favor later this afternoon."

"When? At lunch?"

"This afternoon. I heard you were having drinks with Mr. Safran."

I was annoyed. And I felt used. I didn't ask Levi to have cocktails so that we could talk about Oskar Jacobi. It irked me that I owed him something, and I regretted ever going to his mansion full of strangers.

He was silent the rest of the drive. Propriety obscured the man I had been speaking with like a cloaking device. We approached Lady Bird Lake and passed the bell tower. The Giantess regarded us as we sped by, and I saw Shyla Kearns tottering out of the salon. Just before we passed the industrial district, a police officer turned on his lights and siren.

Jacobi waved out the window and pulled over, retrieving something out of his coat pocket. "Hello, mate." He handed an envelope to the police officer. When he opened it, his face paled in shame.

"My mistake, Mr. Jacobi. It'll be easy to remember this car next time, sir."

Jacobi waved him off, and we sped through the edges of Austin.

"What did you show him?" I asked.

"I bought a million dollars' worth of weapons and riot gear for the Austin Police Department a few years back. The chief of police was kind enough to write me a very nice letter."

With Austin behind us and the river sparkling on our right, we zipped along East Austin, a part of town that only watches people like Jacobi move through it. At nearly every intersection, a white cross, decorated with bright flowers and pictures of a loved one, marked the death spots where someone had been killed in an accident or murdered.

Life is better than this. It's full of possibilities for me.

Even Jacobi was a possibility. It wasn't hard to imagine.

***

Midday bustled with people headed for lunch. We weren't far from the airport. Jacobi pulled up to a quaint bungalow-turned-restaurant called Tristan's. We walked around to the patio. Wooden bistro tables and chairs shaded by white and red umbrellas lined the soft gravel. A large red sign was attached to the side of the building. In white letters, it read TABAC. We had just sat down when a short man with a disproportionately large head and nose took a seat at our table.

"Mr. Iverson, this is Mr. Rosenberg."

He blinked his shrew-like eyes in my direction and shook my hand.

"Should I tell you what I did to that guy?" He was still shaking my hand, faster now.

"What did you do, sir?" I asked.

He withdrew his hand as if mine were on fire. He wasn't speaking to me. He leaned closer to Jacobi, enveloping him with his giant head.

"I told Kaplan, 'Kaplan, don't lift a finger for this guy until he shuts his pie hole.' And that was the end of it."

"Something to drink, gentleman?" asked the waiter.

"This place is a fine brasserie," said Mr. Rosenberg, looking at the green ivy crawling up the trellis. "But where we met last time is more my style."

"Duvel for all of us, if you have it on tap," Jacobi told the waiter. "I didn't like it, Rosenberg. It was too cramped."

"Cramped, yes," said Mr. Rosenberg. "Oy! The times we had there."

"Where are you talking about?" I asked.

"Hoffbrau's."

"Hoffbrau's," whined Mr. Rosenberg. "Some people there we can never meet again. Some friends long buried. Who can forget the night Max Kohn got knifed there? May he rest in peace. We'd been gluttonous pigs and were full of beer, remember, Jacobi? Then the waiter came over. He didn't look right. He tells Max someone's outside, and it's urgent. Max gets up to go, so I grab his arm, and I says, 'Hand to God you go out there, and I'll bust your bloody chops. Let 'em come in here if they need you so bad.'"

"Did he go?" I asked.

"Hell if he didn't." Mr. Rosenberg's forehead nearly collapsed on top of me. "He stopped in the doorway and yelled: 'I'm not done with that beer yet!' Then he walked out, and they stabbed him five times in the neck."

"Did they ever catch them?" I asked.

"Nu? I hear you are looking for a business deal."

I was stunned at the non-sequitur.

Jacobi swooped in:

"Not him. He's not the one."

"He's not?" Mr. Rosenberg folded his arms.

"Mr. Iverson is just a buddy of mine. We'll talk about the thing later."

"Okay, so he's not the guy," said Mr. Rosenberg.

Three glistening plates of *Côtes de Porc* arrived, and Mr. Rosenberg, having recovered from the nostalgia of Hoffbrau's, sliced meat from the bone with finesse. He swallowed the pieces so quickly—and didn't choke—causing me to wonder if his throat were unusually large, like his head. Given over to automatic fressen, his shrewlike eyes were free to inspect the people around our table. I don't think he missed a thing. And I ventured that if I had not been sitting in my chair, he would have gawked under our table for a more grounded view.

"Tell me, mate," said Jacobi, taking hold of my arm. "Did I upset you earlier in the car?"

There was that secure smile again. I pressed my heel into the gravel to fight against his power.

"I don't like puzzles," I said, "and I'm confused why you won't just tell me what you want from me. Why does it have to involve Mr. Safran?"

"I promise I'm not being devious," he said. "Mr. Safran is a professional, and he wouldn't agree to anything untoward."

Jacobi's phone rang, and he hurried from the table.

"Important call, I guess," said Mr. Rosenberg, his eyes watching Jacobi's backside as he stepped inside the bungalow. "He's a real gentleman, is he not? And dead handsome to look at."

"Yes," I said before considering his statement.

"You know he went to Harvard."

"So I've heard. Have you known Jacobi long?" I asked.

"Many years," he said, nodding his head slowly. "And as soon as I met him, I knew I was in the presence of greatness. I said to myself: 'He's the kind of man you wish you could take home to meet *mamaleh*.'" He blinked twice. "You've noticed my ring."

I hadn't noticed it, but his remark drew my eyes. It was brushed silver with a blue diamond.

"The diamond is made from the extracted carbon of cremains," he told me.

"Oh!" I looked closer, mesmerized and a touch concerned. "Whose ashes are they?

Jacobi returned to the table, and as he sat down, Mr. Rosenberg gulped the last of his coffee and stood.

"Lunch has been a pleasure," he said, "and I'll leave you two at it."

"Don't leave just yet, Gabriel," said Jacobi with disinterest.

Mr. Rosenberg waved his hand in protest. "You're very kind, but you young men don't need this relic," said he. "Enjoy the scenery. I've outstayed my welcome."

We shook hands, and his immense head was shaking. I wondered if I had irritated him.

"He gets that way sometimes," said Jacobi. "Mushy. This is one of those days. But he's quite the philanthropist. Especially to the arts."

"What's his story? Was he an actor?"

"Not at all."

"A lawyer?"

"Gabriel Rosenberg?" Jacobi chuckled. "No, he's a fixer."

"What do you mean?"

"Let's just say the old man is a cunning problem solver. He has a way of making people get along."

"How did he get into that business?" I asked.

"He started running with the Jewish mafia in New York, and then moved on to Cleveland but relocated again and found Texas a suitable hub to work from."

"The Jewish mafia?"

"Didn't know about that, did you, mate?"

The concept had never occurred to me, but if I thought there were such a thing, I might have dismissed it as a conspiracy theory or even an antisemitic notion.

"Has Mr. Rosenberg ever been to prison?"

"Not a chance. He's too smart to get caught," said Jacobi.

When the waiter brought the bill, I reached for my card. Before I could lay it on the table, Jacobi put his hand over mine. He kept it there while handing his card to the young man. And then he lowered our hands onto my knee, his smooth, warm fingers interlaced with mine. I blushed and looked around the patio. When I saw Fallon Macandeior coming out of the bungalow, I pulled my hand out from under his.

"Come with me for a second," I said. "I want to say hello to someone."

Fallon noticed us and changed directions. She galloped toward our table.

"So you are still alive," said Fallon. "Donovan is pissed because you never come over."

"Fallon, this is Mr. Jacobi."

Jacobi became clumsy. He nearly knocked a glass off the table when he stood to shake her hand. The skin around his lips was tight and pale.

"What have you been doing all this time?" asked Fallon. "And why did you have to come so far to eat?"

"To have lunch with Mr. Jacobi."

I turned to say something to him, but he was gone.

* * *

One October day in two thousand fifteen—

(said Levi that afternoon, sitting with one leg over his knee in Lutie's bar at the Commodore Perry Estate)

—I was taking a stroll across the tree lawns because the grass was so thick it cushioned my feet. My scarf flapped in the wind just like the nylon flags on all the houses serving me tsk tsks when I passed by.

The biggest house with the most prominent flag was Donovan's. He was twenty, just a year and a half older than me, and was the hottest boy in Columbus, hunty. He made tongues wag; it didn't matter if they were boys or girls. He wore a blazer and shorts and had a sporty convertible and was on the phone all day, every day.

When I walked by his house that morning, his car was parked at the curb, and he was inside with a man I had never seen before. They were so into each other Donovan didn't see me until I was right up on his car.

"Hey, Levi," he said. "Come here."

I admit I was surprised he wanted to speak to me right then. He asked me if I was going to the ball field. I told him I was. And then he asked if I would let the guys know he wasn't going to make it that day. The older man watched Donovan while he was talking to me. He was smiling like there was nothing else in the world. I don't care much for other people's affairs, darling, but this was so fierce I'll never forget it. The man's name was Oskar Jacobi, and I wouldn't see him again until Emerald Bluff. The first time we ran into each other at a party, I didn't realize it was the same man.

By two thousand sixteen, I had my share of boys chasing me, and I was competing in more fights, so I didn't see Donovan much. Then the dish started on Facebook that his parents caught him sneaking out to go see some older man. The rumors must've been true. He was locked in his room for weeks. And after that drama, he didn't hook up with men anymore, only with girls—some younger, some older.

His parents tried to set him up with a chick from Pennsylvania, but in June, he married Fallon. It was probably the most lavish wedding Columbus had ever seen before. Fallon invited hundreds of people and booked the first two floors of the Westin, and the day before they tied the knot, she gave him a three-million-dollar Bugatti Chiron.

I was his best man. I went to his room an hour before the rehearsal dinner. He was sprawled out on the bed in his tux, drunk as a skunk. He had a bottle of scotch in one hand and a letter in the other.

"Aren't you so happy for me," he mumbled.

"What the fuck's wrong with you, Donovan?"

I'd never seen a boy like that before. He scared me.

"Here, my love." He fumbled in a trash can next to him on the bed and fished out the keys to the Bugatti. "Darling, take these to Fallon and tell everyone Donovan's changed his mind. Say: 'Don Don's changed his mind.'"

He started sobbing. And sobbing. I ran out and found his daddy, and we got him in a cold bath. He took that letter into the bathtub and clutched it to his chest. He finally let me put it in a drawer after it got all soggy.

Then he was quiet as a synagogue mouse. We put a cold towel on his neck, made him drink coffee, and then got him back in his tux and walked him to the dining hall. The next day he married Fallon Macandeior without a hitch, bitch. After that, they left to go on a Mediterranean cruise.

The next time I saw them in August, Donovan seemed crazy about her. If she left even for a minute, he'd grab my arm and look around: "Where did Fallon go?" he'd ask. He looked like a lost puppy until she came back. He'd lay his head in her lap and trace her face with his fingers. It was like watching monkeys grooming lice off each other.

Not a month later, Fallon had a wreck late at night. The boy with her broke his neck, paralyzed. It was all over the news.

Donovan never said a word about it to me, and I wasn't about to bring it up.

Then Fallon had their son, and they left the country for a year to travel. I saw them in Munich and again in Rome. They finally came to Austin to settle down. Donovan is popular here. You know that. He's damn good-looking. And there's the wealth, the house, the cars; everyone loves him. And I never hear anyone talking bad about him. Maybe because Fallon absorbs the worst. If things get weird, Donovan can just shut up and let Fallon talk; then everybody's blind to his own shit.

Long story longer, about six weeks ago, he heard Jacobi's name for the first time in ages. It was when I asked you if you knew Jacobi. Do you remember? After you left that night, Donovan came in, woke me up, and said: "What Jacobi are you talking about?" Half asleep, I told him what he looked like. "My Jacobi," he said in a far-off way. Then I knew that this Jacobi was the man in Donovan's little convertible way back when.

* * *

When Levi finished his story, we left the Commodore Perry and drove around Zilker Park. The sun had set behind the hills to the west, and only joggers and tennis players occupied the park.

"What are the odds Jacobi and Donovan ended up living near each other?" I asked. "It's bizarre."

"It's not a coincidence, darling."

"What?"

"Jacobi built that mansion on Emerald Bluff so Donovan would be right across the river."

It wasn't just the fountain of Apollo that Jacobi had been reaching out to that June night. Suddenly, he became three-dimensional to me, rendered completely beyond the man in the mansion.

"Carry, he wants you to ask Donovan to come to your cottage one afternoon, and then he'll pop by."

This request, liaised through Levi, astounded me. Jacobi had pined away all these years for Donovan and then built a mansion to host every debauchery—so that he could "pop over" to my cottage. I swallowed down my anger (looking back, I realized I was sorely jealous).

"Why the fuck didn't he just ask me himself?"

"He's scared, hon. Scared that Donovan's not interested in him anymore. Scared of hurting you."

I was concerned, mainly about that last part.

"So why not just ask you to make the connection?"

"And waste that glorious house of his? Jacobi wants Donovan to see it," he said. "And your little cottage is next door."

"I see."

"When Donovan and Fallon weren't showing up at his parties, Jacobi began asking around if people knew him. And then he found me!" Levi fanned his face as if he were having a hot flash. "Remember that party when he brought me into the library? Gurl, you should have seen how nervous he was. He stammered and dodged, so I suggested the two of them go for lunch in Austin. I thought he was going to pull his hair out. He had one way this was going to go, and I hadn't caught his vision yet."

"'I need to make this as easy on Donovan as I can,' Jacobi told me. 'It has to be next door at Carry's.'"

"When I told him you had gone to college with Fallon, he started to reconsider his plan."

We drove out of the park, and I put my arm around Levi's shoulder and pulled him toward me. I asked him if he wanted to have dinner, and then I wasn't thinking about Donovan and Jacobi anymore, but only of this hardened, lonely person who fit perfectly in the crook of my arm. A quote drummed in my head that aroused me: "In this world, we can love, we can long, and we can lose; but, we cannot stop."

"Donovan deserves to be happy," said Levi.

"Does he want to see Jacobi?"

Levi covered his lips with his finger. "He can't know about the plan. Jacobi doesn't want him to know. Just invite him over."

We turned off the highway onto a tree-lined road. Then Austin's blue, green, and golden skyline pierced the sky. Unlike Jacobi and Fallon, I didn't have a boy whose specter haunted the dark surface of the water and the putrid underbelly of the city, and so I pulled the boy next to me close. His thin, mocking mouth smiled, and so I drew him up closer, this time to my lips.

We stopped at a row of food trucks and devoured two plates of fajitas, sitting at a bench under a large oak with oversized holiday lights.

"Let's go to the hotel," said Levi without looking at me. He glanced at me sideways and put his hand on my thigh when I didn't answer. "Pretty please?"

"Should we pick up something for drinks on the way?"

"There's a fully stocked bar, hon. I don't think you'll go thirsty," said Levi.

He had a room at The Line, the hotel that hosted the Giantess's enormous face and eyes. I made a move toward the chic bar across the lobby, but Levi locked his arm in mine and said we would order something up. He led me to the elevators. When the bell indicated ours had arrived, my stomach sank. Levi had never brought up being trans. I ignored the nagging ambiguity of the situation and decided to take it one step at a time. There was still the reprieve of booze.

"Call the bar, love. I want something strong," said Levi, turning on a red lamp that looked like inflamed genitalia.

I ordered a bottle of bourbon. Levi had made his way to the sectional after opening the curtains and sat down.

I vacillated between saying something to him before the waiter arrived and giving him time to tell me in his own way. I plopped down next to him and leaned on one of the high-backed black sectionals.

"You look nervous," said Levi, running his fingers through my hair.

"Do I? I can't imagine why."

"Maybe I intimidate you," he said.

Someone knocked.

"I'll be right back," said Levi. "Take your shoes off or something. Get comfy."

I watched Levi walk to the door. His movements were slick and choreographed. I slipped off my shoes. My pulse pounded in my ear.

"Do we do it the civilized way or are you up for something more unrefined?" asked Levi.

My body flinched. "What do you mean?"

"The bourbon, honey. Do you want glasses, or can we just share the bottle?"

"I don't mind sharing," I said.

I thought to ask him about the championship he won but lost in Israel, but he mounted my lap and unbuttoned my shirt, running his fingers over my chest. I pulled his sweater over his short, wild, black hair. His tongue probed my teeth and throat as his hand crept beneath my waistband. I let my finger trace a faint scar under his chest. He didn't react. So I moved to the other side, finding his nipple and the other scar.

"Would you like to ask me something?" he pulled his hand out of my pants. His breath was hard and wet against my lips.

"When were you going to tell me?" I asked.

"I'm telling you. Now, like this."

I froze because the rules had changed at that moment. How much did I want to know?

He must have read my confusion: "I still have a pussy. But I'm a man, Carry. Can you understand that?"

"I'm trying."

He edged off my lap and leaned his head against my shoulder. "The top surgery went well. I love how I look. The rest is happening next year."

"You mean—" I hesitated. "You're getting a—"

"A dick, hon. Yes, I'll have the whole package. And the outside will match the inside. You get that?"

"I get it. And I see that you're a man. But I don't understand why you kept this from me."

"You think I want to go around and announce to everybody that they should please excuse the pussy, but I'm really a boy?"

"That's absurd. But you might want to have a conversation about it before you get around to fucking someone."

"Who says we're fucking?"

"Don't deflect, Levi. I don't know how to talk about this. Have some patience with me." I stood up and leaned my head against the window. The glass was cold. The hills around Lake Travis shimmered with lights—people in their homes doing everyday things: washing dishes, taking the trash out, bingeing Netflix—while the air in the room felt foreign, as though I were an alien trying to acclimate to a new world.

"Let me help you," said Levi.

He took my hand, and we walked into the bedroom. He pushed me down on the bed and had unfastened my belt and pulled my pants off before I could think about our next moves.

"What about you?" I asked, meaning his clothes. "Do you want—"

"Stop talking." Levi stepped out of his pants, leaving on his tight, red boxers. Before he turned out the light, I noticed a bulge and locked onto his eyes. "I pack, baby. Now relax."

He crawled on top of me, and I wrapped my arms around him. His skin was warm and smelled of bergamot and sage. He started rubbing his sex against mine. He kissed me hard. Ecstasy overpowered confusion, and I merged with his rhythm. He slipped under the covers, between my thighs, and I whispered his name.

I have no life but this,
  To lead it here;
  Nor any death, but lest
  Dispelled from there;
  Nor tie to earths to come,
  Nor action new,
  Except through this extent,
  The realm of you.

Emily Dickinson

Chapter Five

I panicked when I made it back to Emerald Bluff later that night. The entire northern end of the cape was cast in red and yellow fiery light. I was afraid my cottage was on fire. A surreal glow flickered over the trees and the shrubs. But when I pulled into my driveway, I saw that it was Jacobi's house, decked with lights from the balconies to the patios and into the garden.

I figured it was another party, a special occasion, maybe one of the elite's birthdays. But it was silent over there. As I stepped out of my SUV, Jacobi was walking toward me across his garden.

"Your house looks like a Griswold Christmas," I said.

"Too much?" He turned his head over his shoulder and smirked. "I kind of admire it. Let's go for a drive, mate."

"It's getting late."

"How about a swim, then? I haven't used either pool all summer."

"All right. Let me get out of these clothes."

"You know, I haven't been skinny dipping since I was in Europe. I dare you, mate."

Two thoughts split my brain: Jacobi naked with me in the pool, and what was he up to?

"Race you," he said. He bolted, undressing as he ran.

I jogged from my yard to his garden and then walked the rest of the way. I was still deciding whether this was a good idea.

Jacobi's lithe, tan body reflected all the light around him. He was standing at the edge of the pool in a diving pose. I noticed his wealth was not the only area where he had been blessed. I took off my clothes and followed him into the pool. Firelight shimmered on the surface. The enchanted warm water, his smile, and the vulnerability of it all opened me. He slid under the water and resurfaced inches from me.

"Do you like this, mate?"

"Of course. It's relaxing."

He moved closer.

"How about this? Still relaxed?"

He looked at my parted lips, and then my eyes.

"I think so. Hard to tell from this distance."

Jacobi waded closer until I could feel him below, stiff and absolute.

"That's definitely clearer."

"Can I kiss you?" he asked.

"If you have to ask—"

"It seems polite," Jacobi said.

"You already know you can—"

He put his hands around my neck and kissed my forehead and chin, and then my throat and shoulder. My face was iron hot. Everything went quiet inside, and I let myself experience him: his tongue, his aromatic breath, his hand cupping me below the water, and his overwhelming sanguinity. I returned his caresses with an appetite. I was stricken with skin-hunger. He pushed against me and dove underwater. Suddenly his hands were clutching my waist, and his legs were wrapped around my ankles. He pushed and pulled his face into my cock against the weight of the water, sending ripples to the edge of the pool.

I thrust into his mouth. My body squeezed and shuddered.

Jacobi came up out of the water and then he kissed me again. I explored his teeth with my tongue. He tasted salty from me along the ridges of the roof of his mouth. Jacobi slid a finger down my ass and I strained to meet it, to bring him inside. But those thoughts of his which drifted in the flotsam of the lake of his mind surfaced.

"Donovan," he sighed.

I shoved him and got out. I wrapped one of the robes around me left for us by the butler. Jacobi emerged from the pool and sat down beside me, ignoring the other robe.

"Are you all right, mate?"

"No, I'm not, " I said. "What about Donovan? Why would you do that to—"

"Carry, it doesn't mean anything. I thought it would cheer us up."

It meant something to me. Jacobi meant something to me. I wanted him, miserably and wholeheartedly, and nothing else could satisfy that want. But I wouldn't let myself be used. Disgust and envy were unfamiliar tendencies, but here they were churning in my stomach.

"Levi mentioned your plan. You should have been straight with me and had the balls to talk to me instead of Levi."

Jacobi propped his head against his fist. "You're right. I've hurt you, and I'm sorry. I like you, Carry. You're intelligent, and an idealist, and a handsome one, too. I think you understand me."

"I don't understand you luring me over here for a dip in your pool when the one you're really after is Donovan." Jacobi moved to put his hand on my shoulder. "I'm going to bed," I said, pulling off the robe. "I'll call Donovan in the morning and invite him."

"Forget about it, mate. I can see this has made you all salty."

"I'm not jealous, and I'm not doing this for you. I'm doing it for Donovan. When is this get-together going to happen?"

"Whenever works for you best."

"The day after tomorrow, then," I said. I wanted this to be over with as soon as possible.

Jacobi considered it and then raised a finger in the air. "I want to clean up the lawn and such."

We looked at the border of our properties—there was a clear division where my weed-infested wilderness stopped, and his meticulous garden started. It was obvious *whose* lawn he was referring to.

"There's one other issue I wanted to bring up," he said.

I was still standing in front of him, leafless. "What, you need more time than that?"

"It's not about Donovan. Insomuch as—" He stood and put his hands on his hips, hesitating. "You wouldn't mind an extra source of income, would you?"

I didn't answer.

"You could afford a better car and update your wardrobe.

"Get to the point," I said.

"I was thinking—I had an idea that could be very profitable for you, as a way of saying thank you for helping me out."

"I'm not helping *you*, Oskar."

"Never mind me, then. I just have a side deal going on which might interest you. It's not time-consuming at all, but it needs to stay on the down-low."

Recalling his offer now, after everything that had happened before he suggested it, gives me great relief because I do believe I dodged a hideous proposal.

"No, I'm too busy with work to take on something else."

"It doesn't involve Rosenberg if that's what you're afraid of." He must have assumed Mr. Rosenberg repulsed me, but I informed him that Rosenberg had nothing to do with my response. He searched my face for an indication that I would say more, but I stared back at him blankly, too wounded to do anything else. He nodded, and we each walked away to our homes.

As I lie in bed that night a thought rotated around my brain: I had forfeited my place among the angels to live among the Sodomites.

* * *

I called Donovan from the office the next morning and invited him over for drinks.

"Fallon is not invited," I told him.

"What are you talking about?"

"Don't bring Fallon. That's what I mean."

"Who is this 'Fallon'?" he asked playfully.

The day couldn't have arrived soon enough. A thunderstorm dumped rain without end. Mid-morning, a man in a black slicker, pushing a lawnmower, knocked on my door.

"Mr. Jacobi sent me to cut the grass."

"Fine," I said and closed the door.

Achilles rubbed against my leg and then ran to his dish. I gave him a can of sardines and remembered I didn't have any liquor, so I drove the market to search for Laphroaig, shot glasses, flowers, and hoagies.

I had no need to buy the flowers. At two o'clock, a florist arrived from Jacobi's in a truck with dozens of arrangements that he began to place in what must have seemed strategic locations. An hour later, Jacobi, wearing a shimmering blue Bergdorf Goodman suit, a freshly pressed white shirt, and a gold tie, let himself in. The dark circles under his eyes suggested he hadn't slept well.

"How is everything?" he asked without greeting me.

"The yard has been cut if that's what you're referring to."

"The yard?" He pushed the curtains open. "Oh, that yard. Looks good, mate." His voice sounded as though it were coming from far up in his head, distant and unsure.

"Very, very good."

"Isn't this all a bit extra?" I asked him.

"He's going to love it. Won't he?" Jacobi didn't wait for an answer. "The news said the rain is supposed to stop around four. Do you have everything as in—as in what to drink?"

I took the Laphroaig out of the cupboard and handed the bottle to him. He turned it around and said, "Shame. I have a Macallan Millennium at home." We moved over to the table and inspected the hoagies from the deli.

"Are these to your liking?" I asked.

"Yes! They're wonderful. Just great!" His voice trailed off as he whispered, "...mate."

The torrent slowed and then was gone by three-thirty, leaving only the soaked trees to pitter-patter onto the tamed grass. Jacobi flipped through a Forbes magazine with deserted eyes, occasionally looking at the floors and inspecting the furniture as if a pile of unforgivable dust had accumulated unawares. He jumped to his feet and announced with great ambivalence that he was going home.

"Why?"

"He's not coming. It's late, and he's not coming for drinks." He checked his watch as if he needed to be somewhere else. "I can't wait all day."

"You're being ridiculous. And a simp. Sit down. It's not even four."

He collapsed as if I had punched him and set his elbows on his knees, resting his chin in his hand. Just then, there was the roar of an engine, and then a screech as a car turned into my driveway. Jacobi jumped up, and I walked out the front door.

"Is this really where you live, darling cousin?"

The invigorating undulation of Donovan's voice was a staccato blast in the damp air. I had to listen for the rests and the beats to comprehend any words. A wet curl of hair lay like a bass clef across his forehead.

"Are you going to seduce me, Carry Iverson?" he asked into my ear. "Why else couldn't I bring Fallon?"

"That's the mystery of *Nights of Awe*. Now let's not keep the whiskey waiting."

We walked inside. The living room was empty.

"Huh, that's unusual," I said.

"What's unusual?"

There was a polite knocking at the door. I opened it. Jacobi was a corpse, stiff as though rigor mortis had set in, his hands flat against his sides for eternity. He shook his shoes out of the puddle, seeking relief in my eyes.

Hands still clamped to his thighs, he crept past me into the hall, made a tight turn as if he were performing a drill, and walked into the living room. It was pathetic. I closed the door loudly in protest.

Quiet. The hush seemed to last forever. Then I heard voices and a laugh and Donovan's contrived tone: "What a pleasure to see you again."

More cruel silence. There was no point in standing in the hall, so I went into the room.

Jacobi's hands hadn't moved. He was leaning against a wall trying to give off a casual air or even disinterest. He leaned his head so far back it knocked a painting off-center. He looked down at Donovan who was sitting on the edge of the sofa, panicked but composed.

"I've seen you at my parties lately," Jacobi said to me. He shifted his eyes toward me and winked, the way a person does when they want to appear confident. The painting pitched further as he pressed his head against it, and then it popped off the wall. It landed in his shaking hands, and he placed it back on the wall askew. He sat down on the sofa, making sure not to disrupt it, too. Finally, his hands had moved from his sides and were folded in his lap.

"Sorry about that painting, mate."

My neck and face were prickling. I searched my brain for a bromide, but they seemed to have deserted me.

"It's not worth anything," I told them as if I knew.

I think we all assumed it had crashed to the floor and shattered.

"We haven't seen each other in years," Donovan said to Jacobi as a *fait accompli.*

"It will be five years in November, precisely."

Jacobi's Spock-like tone derailed us all again. I suggested the Laphroaig and hoagies hoping to break the ice.

The glasses clinking, the pouring, the cutting, the passing of plates, and the routine of manners made for a much-needed diversion. Jacobi stuffed himself into a corner and, while Donovan and I talked, he bounced his attention between us, trying to appear interested, but there was no cure for his douchebaggery. I excused myself and headed to the hall.

"Where are you going?" asked Jacobi

"I won't be long."

"We need to talk about—to discuss an important matter."

He clipped at my heels and followed me into the kitchen, closed the door, and grabbed my face. "Fuck, this was a mistake!"

"Pull yourself together. The two of you just need to recover from the lost time. And this would be awkward for anyone." I sounded sincere, but I didn't believe that.

"You think that's how he feels?" he asked.

"Of course."

"Keep it down!"

I'd lost my patience by now. "You're acting childish, Oskar. And impolite. And weird. You've left Donovan by himself."

He pointed his finger at me and looked into my eyes with severe admonishment. I jabbed my elbow into his arm and opened the door. Jacobi went back to the living room, and I walked out the back door. It was pouring again. Under the giant oak, whose branches and leaves formed a canopy with its siblings, I observed my yard. Jacobi's gardener had cut it too close, and now a meshwork of mires concealed his overzealous efforts.

Jacobi's mansion took possession of my attention, and I stared at it, reminded of Rearden's home in Rand's novel.

It was sunny after about an hour, but patches of rain refused to surrender. The catering trucks ambled around Jacobi's drive with the goods for the next party. Staff opened doors and windows, likely airing out an imaginary stench, as the place was always spotless. The half-hearted rain stuttered, and I realized the voices from inside the cottage had fallen into a similar rhythm.

I returned to the kitchen, jingling keys, opening and closing the oven door, and slamming the refrigerator shut. I couldn't tell whether my guests noticed. They were sitting on either end of that sofa, silent, staring at each other as if some question had erased all pretenses. Donovan had been crying, and when I walked in, he rubbed his eyes with his hands. But Jacobi had slipped into his familiar personage. From every pore in his golden skin, he radiated a cocksure wildness.

"There you are, mate," he said, as though I'd just returned from a vacation.

"The rain stopped."

"I hadn't noticed." He looked around the room and smiled, posed even with his chest puffed out—Apollo admiring his work. "It has stopped raining, Donovan."

"We all needed it to stop, Oskar." His buoyant voice mismatched the pain in his face.

"Let's all go to my house," he said. "I'd like to show Donovan around."

"I don't need to go," I said.

"Of course, you do, mate. I insist."

Donovan went upstairs to freshen up while Jacobi and I waited in the yard.

"My house is beautiful, isn't it?" he asked, expecting an answer. "Look, Carry, how it catches the light reflecting off the lake."

"Splendiferous," I said. He either didn't catch my sarcasm or ignored it.

"Just beautiful." His eyes traced the curve of the grand foyer, the pillars, and every arch. "It only took me a few years to earn the money to build it."

"You said you inherited money from your family."

"I did, mate," he snapped, "but I squandered most of it."

I think he realized he had made a slip. "How did you earn the money?"

"That is none of your business." He must have realized his severity. "But generally speaking, I've been in pharmaceuticals, private military services, but neither of those now." He looked me over, and I knew what was coming. "Does your sudden interest in my businesses mean you're considering my proposal from the other night?"

Donovan came out of the cottage. "That's your mansion?" he asked.

"What do you think about it?"

"It's exquisite. But you're all alone there, Oskar."

"I am not alone. It's always full of alluring people. VIPs. Only the magnetic."

We took the private road to Jacobi's. Donovan praised the parallaxes of the mansion against the sky; he gushed over the gardens, the sparkling pools, and landscaping. It was eerie to walk up the steps and not see the bright costumes flashing in and out of the door and not hear the pounding music, only the birds calling in the trees.

Inside, we took in the halls, entertainment rooms, and sitting areas. My mind played tricks on me, imagining movement from a guest behind a couch or under a table, as though abiding by Jacobi's order to disappear until we passed by. As Jacobi closed the door to the library, I was sure I saw old raven-eyes mocking us.

We meandered through the bedrooms, all decorated with different themes: nautical, Victorian, bohemian, modern, with their walk-in showers and sunken bathtubs. We interrupted Mr. Pfeffer, the "roommate," exercising on the Nordic Track. At last, we came to Jacobi's suite, an expansive bedroom and bath, and his private office, where we sat and drank the Macallan Jacobi took from his bar.

He watched Donovan taking everything in, as though he valued the worth of every object by the response it evoked from him. His eyes, too, inventoried his riches in a disoriented way, as if the presence of Donovan rendered them all meaningless.

Jacobi's bedroom was the most contemporary. His walk-in closet was as large as a guest room. Donovan walked in and felt the fabrics, picked up shoes, and fingered the racks of ties.

Two disparate emotions flashed across Jacobi's face, first embarrassment and then elation over Donovan's presence. He had fantasized about this moment for so long, dreamt about it, visualized it with such clarity, now that it was unfolding, his core was melting down because Jacobi was an abuser of time: he treated those who cared about him like people he would inescapably lose. And to cushion the impact, which he knew would undoubtedly happen, he rehearsed their exit even while they were still present in his life.

"Can you believe I have a clothing mentor? He brings over selections at the beginning of every season."

He brought out a pile of shirts and tossed them on the bed, one by one: silks, linens, flannels, all in colors fit for winter, spring, and summer. We felt our way through them as he brought out more and the upscale pile grew higher—stripes and plaids in blueberry and orange, each monogrammed. Suddenly, Donovan rolled in the pile and laughed.

"Oskar, your couture is rich handsome realness," he howled. "And it makes me so happy I could gag."

* * *

Finished with the house, we intended to see the gardens, pools, and boat—but the rain returned, so we looked out a window facing the cove.

"If it weren't for the rain, we could see your home across the river," said Jacobi. "Apollo always radiates from the top of your hill."

Donovan took his hand, but Jacobi gazed across the river as if searching for the fountain. I wondered if he now thought that the gravity of that statue had lost its meaning. Donovan had been so out of reach, but Apollo had kept watch over him. Now it was just marble and metal constructed on a hill—one less treasure for Jacobi to accumulate.

In the half-light, a portrait of an older man attracted my attention.

"Who is this?"

"Him? That's Morty Foster, mate."

The name rang a bell.

"He's dead now. He was my closest friend many years ago."

On a desk, there was a small black and white photograph of Jacobi, full of vim, on a boat with Mr. Foster—Jacobi seated between the man's legs with his hand holding on to Foster's and looking about sixteen.

"I love the hair," said Donovan. "You never told me you had a shaggy swoop."

Jacobi's cell rang.

"I can't speak at the moment, mate…I said a small venue… Doesn't he know what that means? Well, what good is he if he thinks that is a small venue…"

He threw the phone on his desk.

"Look at this," said Donovan, standing at the window.

The rain was falling softly now, but golden light had opened up above the lake.

"I want to be out there with you, on your boat," he said.

I made my move to leave them to themselves, but they wouldn't allow it; maybe with me as the third wheel, they felt they could be closer.

"I've got an idea," said Jacobi.

He left the room calling for John and returned in a few minutes with a disgruntled young guy with a buzz cut wearing a tie-dyed t-shirt, khaki shorts, and Birkenstocks.

"Did we interrupt you?" asked Donovan.

"I was sleeping," whined Mr. Pfeffer. "Well, I had been sleeping until—"

"Pfeffer plays the piano," said Jacobi. "Don't you, John."

"Sort of. But I'm out of prac—"

"Let's go downstairs," said Jacobi.

He called for his butler to prepare the lounge. The room was lit by a single soft light shining on the piano. The tables had lamps that flickered with candlelight and cast a trinity of circles in the center. We sat at a table near the back in a dark corner. Jacobi kept his hand steady enough to light Donovan's cigar with an antique, golden lighter.

Pfeffer played a light jazz song, searching the room for Jacobi in the shadows.

"This is shit. I haven't played in so long. I'm all out of—"

"Don't talk, mate, " said Jacobi. "Just play."

Thunder growled across the lake. People were turning on the lights in their houses on Emerald Bluff, and the stream of cars bringing workers home from Austin plodded through the rain. It was a time of intense transition, and possibility was in the air.

I made another attempt to leave and, as I said goodbye, that look of disorientation returned to Jacobi's face as though he distrusted his present achievement. During those five years when they were absent from each other's lives, and even this afternoon,

Donovan surely fell short of Jacobi's expectations—by no fault of his own, but because of Jacobi's burdensome clarity of vision. The Donovan imagined had outgrown the Donovan the real. Like a painter, Jacobi had put everything into his creation, adding a stroke here and mixing a color there. For no truth or sentiment can defy the illusions we store in our wraithy hearts.

Jacobi held onto Donovan's hand, and as he whispered something in Jacobi's ear, he turned toward him with a surge of passion. I think Donovan's voice captivated him the most; with its animated warmth, it couldn't be fabricated—that voice was an imperishable vibration.

They no longer were aware of me. Jacobi had wiped me from his memory. I took one last look at them, and they glanced my way, seeing through me; they vibrant with life, and I an apparition lost in the fug of the room. I left the lounge and went down the steps into the storm, leaving them there together.

Peaceful wealth, or painful toil,
Chance of war, or civil broil,
'Tis not for man's feeble race
These to shun, or those embrace.
But that all-disposing Fate
Which presides o'er mortal state,
Where it listeth, casts its shroud
Of impenetrable cloud.

Bacchylides

Chapter Six

One morning, a gutsy reporter from the *Statesman* arrived at Jacobi's door.

"Mr. Jacobi, would you like to make a comment?"

"About what?" asked Jacobi.

"Anything to clear the air about you."

"Madam, you are claiming that there is a tiny china teapot orbiting the sun. I have no interest in proving otherwise. Good day."

It turns out that the woman had overheard Jacobi's name around her office. She had connected him to something of a scandal, she thought, but wouldn't give any details. She said she had come out of "a courtesy" to Jacobi.

Anyone with an ear to the ground could have picked up the story. Jacobi's fame had been the talk of his guests on Facebook, Twitter, and Instagram, each feeling they had the true story about his past. Accusations of human trafficking surrounded him, and one rumor, in particular, gained traction: the mansion wasn't Jacobi's after all, and that he lived out of an RV, traveling from city to city only to rent a house for his wassails. I never understood why these tall tales gave Oskar Jakobovits of Minnesota so much pleasure.

Oskar Jakobovits—that was his name at birth. He had legally changed it when he was seventeen when his life changed forever on account of meeting Morty Foster. It was Oskar Jakobovits who had been lingering around the parking lot that day in dirty khaki pants and a shabby green hoodie, but it was Oskar Jacobi who approached Foster's Cadillac Escalade and told him that a good sanding and new paint would protect it from the road salt in the winter.

I think he attached the name to himself long before that. His parents were struggling farmers, and in his mind, they weren't his parents at all—they were just people he had to put up with. The reality is, Oskar Jacobi of Emerald Bluff, Texas, stuffed Oskar Jakobovits of Minnesota inside a magic black box and made him disappear. Freed of his past, Jacobi became like Kronos, son of Gaia and Ouranos, and leader of the Titans. He accumulated perverse powers and hungered after extravagance and beauty—the archetype a teenage boy would invent, and a persona Jacobi maintained to the end.

Jakobovits had lived this way for a year in Minneapolis, working odd jobs like biking to and from offices as a courier, washing dishes, doing masonry work at construction sites; whatever could earn him enough for food and shelter. He had an eye for older men who he knew would spoil him only to end up resenting them for it. He hated boys his age because they were clingy and going nowhere. Everyone else he disdained because they were short-sighted and served him no purpose.

But his soul was tormented. Lustful and extravagant fantasies played in his mind at night. An unspeakable sumptuous world materialized while the sun passed over the underbelly of the earth, and the filthy light of the city stained his clothes crumpled on the floor. Every night he added details to his creation until sleep blackened his three-dimensional diorama as if to give blessing to his labor. This castle-building was not a product of a healthy imagination but an adumbration of his delusion, a divination that his grasp on reality was as thin as tissue paper.

As a practical step toward his life of success, he enrolled in a community college in western Minnesota a few months before his fateful meeting with Foster. He was there less than three weeks, bitter that no one had recognized his greatness and resentful of his campus job at the library, which had been given to him to offset tuition. After leaving college, he came to Minneapolis to discover the next rung on the prominence ladder. It was there he encountered Morty Foster and his rusty Cadillac.

Foster was forty-nine years old at the time. He'd grown up near the area that would become known as Silicon Valley and rode the wave of technology that helped create Apple and Microsoft. His ground-floor investments made him millions, but a long line of pretty, savvy boys were happy to take it from him. One, in particular, Allen Edevane, was the smooth felling-stone of David and put Foster out to pasture. To recover, Foster started his own arbitrage firm and wandered the country for years buying stock in companies he knew were takeover targets. Before the leveraged buyout was announced, the stock prices skyrocketed, and he sold the shares for a profit. He was on one of these foraging trips when he pulled into Minneapolis and caught Oskar Jakobovits' eye.

To the young Jakobovits, living hand to mouth, sleeping in a sleazy motel, seeing Foster in his slick suit and expensive car represented the success he was after. Maybe he gave Foster one of his winning smiles—by then, he'd learned you could get people to do things for you if you smiled. Foster talked him up, paid him attention, and noticed the ambition in the boy. He bought him a business suit, a stylish pair of loafers, and when Foster rolled out of town, Jacobi went with him.

Foster gave Jacobi inflated job titles for when they met with potential customers. First, he was Foster's secretary, and then office administrator, and even chief image officer, for the sober Morty Foster had a handle on what the whiskey-bibber Morty Foster could get into. He mitigated this damage by giving Jacobi more responsibility.

Theirs was a Whitman-Doyle relationship that lasted five years. They traveled the world together for business and pleasure. The two might have been together longer if Allen Edevane had not confronted them in Los Angeles, and a week later, Morty Foster had dropped dead.

That photograph of Foster hanging in Jacobi's bedroom was a mystery to me until later. He was a tall, slender, long-faced man with a capacious smile and perfect white teeth. His cropped salt and pepper hair gave him a clean, boy scout-honest look. But the intrepid hedonist embraced that American phase of nineteenth-century old New York by seeking out dives that were the modern-day versions of Armory Hall in the Bowery. Foster was such a sot—at parties, he would have young men rub his feet with champagne—and Jacobi had to remain sober to watch over him. This temperance became a habit, and the habit became a part of Jacobi.

Jacobi was to inherit all of Foster's wealth—an estate worth millions of dollars. But he never saw all of it. Allen Edevane employed a team of lawyers to concoct a scheme proving he alone was Foster's successor. Edevane gave Jacobi one million dollars as "pity money" (Edevane would have known well what Foster put him through) and made him promise to stay far away from him. He left the affair with ample startup money, and the amorphous image of the boy Oskar Jacobi conjured had solidified into the sinister shape of the man he had grown into.

* * *

Jacobi told me this story much later, but I think it belongs here for the purpose of shattering the fantastical notions of his origin story, which were all lies. You see, I had just begun to believe his counterfeit account—and had admitted to myself that I loved him—when he revealed this history, banishing any leeway I had given him. So it's fitting to digress at this point because that is precisely what Jacobi did next.

And it was a vast digression regarding my interactions with him. We didn't see each other or speak on the phone for many weeks. I was mostly running around with Levi, trying to figure out what I felt for him.

We took a trip out to the Hill Country. Levi wanted to visit a winery, so we chose Ab Astris in Stonewall. Then we made our way into Fredericksburg and ate lunch at the Auslander, where there was no shortage of beer and knockwurst. Boozy and torpid, we decided to book a cabin at the A-Frame Ranch. Our two-story lodge gave off a minimalist vibe: black and white furniture and appliances, slate-gray hardwood floors, and a sizable deck with a fire pit. There was a bedroom with a king-size bed downstairs, but we chose the smaller bed in the loft at the top of the A-frame.

We ate a light dinner and then sipped wine on the deck. The sun was below the horizon, offering a parting gift of orange and pink light. Levi's hard face had softened under the tiny golden lights hanging in the trees.

"Is this what you were hoping for?" I asked.

"Darling, a glass of wine on a quaint deck does not an impression make. We could be anywhere."

"How could this be anywhere? There's a reason why it's a popular tourist spot." I tussled his hair, hoping he'd become more playful.

"You have a point. But it's only half of what I want," he said, leaning on his elbow at an angle closer to my face.

"And the other half?"

"You fucking me in that tiny bed upstairs."

I lowered my eyes and stared at the stark grain of the wood on the deck. I noticed a knot that looked like a face with one menacing eye. "I don't know how that works, Levi."

"Did you fail sex-ed in school?"

"Of course, I *know* what you mean. I mean, I think I do. But I've never been with a wom—"

"Full stop. Don't pass go. You've got this all turned around, hon."

I was more confused at this present request than that first easy night when we were together at the hotel Giantess.

"You don't put it in there. *That* is just a body part in this cocoon waiting for the butterfly to come out."

"Oh! You mean—"

"That's right, baby. I want you to take the vein train to A-town." I spewed my wine. Levi wiped a dribble with his thumb from the corner of my lip and licked it slowly.

"I think I've had enough to drink; how about you?" he asked.

He took my glass and walked toward the cabin. "Stay put. I'll just wash these up. I'll call for you when I'm ready."

All at once, I didn't want him to call me in; I wasn't sure *I* was ready. But I remembered his groans from that night, the sounds of him coming. I was horny and scared.

"I'm ready, Carry," he called. My knees shook, but I was hard.

We sat on the little bed facing each other.

"You're trembling. Let's work this out, baby." He took his shirt off and began to unbutton mine. "I think one part of you wants to run up out of here screaming, and another part," he slid his hands in my pants, "wants to come out and play. Am I right?"

He totally had me. And I loved *another part wants to come out and play* that he tossed in strategically. He had noticed everything I was feeling and still wanted me. He licked my lips and then parted them with his soft tongue as if to open my mouth and give expression to the desire and the knots in my stomach at the same time. The thrill and dread took on a different variation of ecstasy. I pulled off the rest of my clothes, and he pushed me onto my back.

"I love to hear your little groans," Levi said. "They make me think this is how you sound when you come. And I like to think about you coming."

"But why?"

"It brings you down to my level, makes you like the rest of us. I want to see your face when I make you come."

"I don't want this to just be one way, Levi."

"If you want, you can play with my clit," he said and turned around to take me in his mouth. "Jerk it like it's a cock, honey."

I felt queasy: I'd never been this close before. His moist, soft petals parted, and he growled with pleasure. He leaned back to give me his ass, and I was relieved by the familiar territory.

After a while, he turned to face me. "You might not love me, Carry, but you need to fuck me."

The next morning, we woke up early, ate a quick breakfast, and drove to Enchanted Rock. The pink granite dome looked like it was illuminated from the inside. People carrying yoga mats were already making their way to the summit.

There are many legends about the formation—once considered a holy portal to other worlds—but the one most people tell is that if you climb to the top with the wrong intentions, either bad luck or death will pursue you.

Levi climbed the steep incline faster than I could. I pretended to watch the translucent fairy shrimp swimming in the vernal pools so I could catch my breath.

"Do you need a rope, slowpoke?"

"You didn't complain about my slow poke last night," I said.

"Oh puh-leeze. Are you a comedian now? Hurry up. My watch says my heart rate isn't even elevated."

We reached the top together. It was cliché, but I took his hand anyway. He squeezed it and said, "Better enjoy the view. It won't last forever."

* * *

I visited Jacobi one Sunday afternoon. I was waiting on his porch and had just found a bench when someone brought Fallon Macandeior over to get a drink. I must have turned pale at seeing her; she looked out of place so near to Jacobi's mansion, like a cowboy firing a pistol at aliens on the moon.

Three of them had been out riding horses—Fallon and a man named Gunnar and a graceful woman whom I recognized from one of the parties.

"So nice to see you," said Jacobi, standing in the doorway. "You've made my day dropping by."

As if Fallon had the capacity to care.

"Come in. Have a cigar." He whispered instructions to the butler. "Drinks are on their way."

Jacobi remained distracted in his role as host; Fallon made him nervous. But Jacobi could never fully relax until he had given his guests the royal treatment, unaware that was exactly what they had come for—to see him perform. Mr. Gunnar wanted no hospitality. A Shiner Bock? I don't drink beer. Champagne then? Too early. How about a coffee? Nothing, thank you.

"How was your ride?"

"Beautiful terrain, really."

"I think the weather has been—"

"Yes, it has."

Possessed by some spirit, Jacobi looked at Fallon, who had tolerated being introduced as though she were a stranger.

"Where have we met before, Mrs. Macandeior?"

"At a luncheon maybe," Fallon said coarsely, but in truth, she had no clue. "Yes, it was that luncheon. I'll never forget it."

"Just a few weeks ago."

"Seems so. It was you and Carry."

"I've met Donovan, you know," pushed Jacobi.

"Is that right? But who hasn't?"

Fallon gestured toward me with her glass: "You live close by, don't you, Carry?"

"I'm Mr. Jacobi's neighbor."

"Seems so."

Mr. Gunnar was mute and looked more like he belonged at Madame Tussauds; the woman was silent until she downed two shots, and then she was quite friendly.

"We would all love to come to your next party, Mr. Jacobi," she said. "Would you invite us?"

"Consider it done. It would be my honor."

"Something to look forward to," said Mr. Gunnar. "Ladies, it's time we headed out."

"But you just arrived," said Jacobi. He had found his center now and wanted to test Fallon. He snapped his fingers. "I know! Why don't you join me for dinner? It's no trouble. There will most likely be others driving in from Austin."

"Let us have *you* for dinner," said the woman. "The both of *you*."

She addressed me. Mr. Gunnar stood up.

"Let's go," he said, taking her arm.

"I'm serious," she said, pulling back against Mr. Gunnar's grip. "It will be so much fun."

Jacobi looked at me as if to ask if I were game, missing the cue from Mr. Gunnar that the invitation did not stand.

"I have plans for the evening," I said.

"Mr. Jacobi? Won't you join us then?"

Mr. Gunnar tightened his grip and whispered something into her ear.

"The evening is young. And if we leave now, there will be plenty of time," she cried.

"I don't have a horse, I'm afraid," said Jacobi. "Never was the type. I'll drive and meet you there. Excuse me for a moment."

We walked out to the driveway where Gunnar and the woman started gesticulating, like a flock of birds preparing to take flight.

"Fuck's sake, he's actually coming," said Fallon. "She has no idea that he's not interested in her."

"She thinks he is."

"She's throwing a party, and he'll be about as popular as a cock in a nunnery." Fallon pulled the scarf around her hair. "Where in the hell did he meet Donovan? They need to keep men like Jacobi in a cage, goddamn pole troller."

Mr. Gunnar called to Fallon from his horse. "Are you ready, Fallon? We're running late. Let's go. And you, boy, tell him we couldn't wait any longer."

We all exchanged half-hearted goodbyes, and they galloped down the driveway past the yellowing leaves and were out of sight just as Jacobi came out the front door in a coyote fur coat.

Fallon must have had a lot to say about Donovan meeting Jacobi, for at the next party, she accompanied him like she was his security detail. Seeing her there seemed to depress everyone. That party I remember more clearly than all the others. The same guests attended, or at least the same types of guests, the same excess of booze, the same neon-bright colors and costumes, the same dramas that played out over and over again, but the air was solemn—much like a room after someone has died—and had never been that way before. Or maybe I was recognizing Jacobi's world as fiction and could no longer suspend my doubts. Perhaps I was grieving something that still looked alive but had long since passed, the way a dead tree stands tall while it rots from the inside out. Jacobi's might-have-been kingdom, with its own rules and majestic figures, was an entity without comparison, for it had no awareness of anything outside of itself. What triggered this shift in perspective was viewing it all through Donovan's eyes. It is distressing to see a thing through new eyes when we work so hard to adjust to it with our own.

They arrived at sunset, and we cruised among the shimmering crowd. Donovan gurgled bizarre vocalizations.

"This is so clutch," he whispered. "If you want to have a scandal, Carry, just tell me, and we'll arrange a kiss in front of a crowd. Or, better yet, hand me a—"

"Take it all in," said Jacobi.

"I am, Oskar. All the lights and sounds—"

"But look into the faces of so many of the people you've heard about."

Fallon's domineering eyes cut across the crowd.

"This isn't my venue normally. I don't know a single person here."

"What about him?" Jacobi pointed to a handsome human anthurium sitting under a Texas persimmon tree. Donovan and Fallon gawked, as people do when they see a movie star in person.

"He's so glamorous," said Donovan.

"The woman standing over him is his agent."

He paraded them from group to group:

"Mr. Macandeior…and Mrs. Macandeior…," and he paused and added, "the equestrian."

Fallon spat her objection: "Don't reduce me to that."

It was too late. The record had broken, and Fallon remained "the equestrian" for the rest of the night.

"This is like the Academy Awards," Donovan said. "I've never seen so many famous people. And she's darling—what was her name?—with the see-through dress?"

Jacobi reminded him, adding that she was only a B-list actress.

"Who cares? She's on her way up!"

"Stop with the 'equestrian' schtick, Jacobi," said Fallon. "I'd rather drink from the River Lethe in Hades than have them remember me as a horse-woman."

Donovan and Jacobi danced. I couldn't take my eyes off him (I'd never seen him dance before), his fiery hips twisting and shaking in a sexy bachata. Then they strolled over to my cottage and sat on the lawn for a long time while I kept watch in the garden per Donovan's request. "In case there's a tornado, darling," he said. "Or God rains hail down, again."

Fallon had returned from Hades as we sat down for dinner. "I'm sitting over there with that guy. He's fucking hilarious."

"Don't choke while you laugh, babe," said Donovan. "And here's a napkin to write down any numbers you might want since you forgot your phone." Donovan scanned the table so as not to be intercepted. "He's handsome, in an average way," he said and I could tell that except for when he was with Jacobi, he was having a miserable time.

We were sitting with a group that had become fairly crocked. It had been my choice—Jacobi had to take a phone call, and I had had a blast with these people at the last party. But we remember most vividly what never took place.

"Are you feeling all right, Miss Briscoe?"

She had been struggling to prop herself up against my shoulder. She jolted upright and tried to look at me.

"Huh?"

A butterball of a man who had invited Donovan to his VIP booth at the racetrack the next day defended Miss Briscoe:

"Hell, she'll be okay. After a few shots, she gets slimy like that. I've tried to introduce her to moderation, but she says she's never met him."

"I do too know him," she slurred.

"You were bellowing so hard that Dr. Saban here heard you clear across the garden."

"It sounded like someone was in pain," said Dr. Saban.

"Yeah, she looks grateful, don't she," said another friend. "You sure fucked her wig up when you forced her head into that fountain."

"I can't—I hate it—the water," said Miss Briscoe. "*They* tried to drown me!"

"Perhaps moderation would be strongly suggested," said Dr. Saban.

"If you started—fffu—fucking off—now...You'd have a—a heads tart," said Miss Briscoe.

The last thing I remember was leaning against Donovan, watching the agent and her actor, still under the persimmon tree, their faces almost touching. I had noticed she'd been inching closer to him all night, and there at that moment, she closed the space between them and kissed his mouth.

"I really do like him," said Donovan. "So handsome."

But the rest of the affair nauseated him. He hated Emerald Bluff, this infestation that Austin had brought upon this Edenic land. He despised its unbridled vitality that chomped at the bit of conventions and its lustful occupants who yearned for a destiny that would always be out of reach. He only saw the gruesome in the very innocence he had lost.

I stood in Jacobi's driveway with them while they waited for their car. The mansion shaded us; only the massive door cast light that could never reach us. Occasionally, a dark figure moved behind a curtain in one of the guest rooms upstairs. Fingers caressed a face. A disembodied hand flicked a cigarette.

"Who really the fuck is Jacobi?" asked Fallon. "A drug dealer, for sure."

"Who told you that rumor?" I asked.

"No one. It just makes sense. So many of the nouveau riche scam their way into wealth."

"Jacobi didn't," I said, realizing my defensiveness only too late.

She was quiet. She put out her cigarette on the pavement, twisting her foot until the butt was flat.

"He's overreaching well beyond his means to put on a spectacle like this."

A gust of wind ruffled Donovan's collar.

"These people have social lives. You have to give them that. More than we can say," he said carefully.

"You looked bored out of your mind, babe."

"I enjoyed myself, darling."

Fallon rolled her eyes and turned to me.

"Did you see the way Donovan's face almost fell to the ground when that woman asked him to help her take a cold shower?"

Donovan hummed with the music, soft at first, and then began singing with a throaty, pulsing vibe, his voice punctuating nuances in the words in a way I'd never heard or would hear again.

"I noticed a lot of people just show up without an invitation," he said. "That woman wasn't invited. I watched their group force their way in, and Jacobi's too much of a gentleman to turn them away."

"Mark my words; he's not right. I'm going to find out who he is," said Fallon.

"You don't have to try very hard, hon. I can tell you all about the drugs," he said.

Fallon's nostrils flared. "Well?"

"He's involved in pharmaceuticals. Lots of them, stateside and overseas."

Their limousine stopped in front of us.

"G'night, Carry darling," said Donovan with a kiss, looking over my shoulder at the brilliance at the top of the steps, where the thrum of a Springsteen tune drifted our way, cautioning us to cherish the time we have. Even in the indifference of Jacobi's party, there was the possibility of intimacy that was unavailable in Donovan's life. What was in that song that begged him to walk back inside? What would he do in the darkness where time stops, or worse, runs backward to the point where it runs out? For Jacobi, some astonishing guest might walk up to him, a man unique among men who could erase the burdens of the last five years with just a smile.

Why couldn't that man be me?

Jacobi asked me to stay until all the guests left. I waited in the garden until the lights in the guest rooms went out. He hurried down the steps, his golden skin taut, his eyes heavy with angst.

"He hated it," he said.

"He said he enjoyed it."

"I know he hated it," said Jacobi through his teeth. "He didn't enjoy it."

I didn't need training as a therapist to see the weight of his depression.

"I feel like I'm drifting away from him," he said. "I can't make him see it."

All he wanted was for Donovan to tell Fallon it was over and say: "I've only loved him." And with that confession, decimate the years he wasted with her so they could make plans to continue their lives together. The first step would be to return to Columbus and get married, just as they should have been five years ago.

"He just can't see it," Jacobi said. "He used to see it. We'd talk about it for hours—"

He stood and paced over half-broken glasses, half-eaten shrimp, and crumpled napkins.

"You're putting a lot on him," I said. "You can't bring back what might have been or rescue things that went away and probably aren't coming back."

He spun around in a fit. "Can't bring back what might have been?" he yelled. "Of course, you can!"

He zigzagged over the garden as if lost time were here, under the table, or there, behind the tree, almost within his reach.

"I'll bring it all back, just the way it was," he said, spitting. "Then he'll see."

Jacobi spoke of things that could have happened but never did with the conviction that they still might. He wanted to live the life that had been wrecked on the rocks of time. He could not let go of this life, which he felt fate still owed him, because the life we insist on living and cannot goes on forever and will not leave us because it never existed in the first place.

… Five years ago, on a fall evening, they were walking down the street. The leaves were falling. They stopped at a treeless place, and the sidewalk was blue from the full moon. They turned to each other. The cool Ohio air carried that passionate adventure between and around them, that crisp potentiality that comes with the change of seasons. The gentle streetlights glowed as if to warm them and to welcome them as if to say: *You belong here.* Jacobi noticed the sharp edges of the sidewalk as it narrowed and disappeared up the hill. To him, it was a ladder to a heavenly place where prayers ascend and blessings descend. If he were alone, he could climb to the source and there receive all of his portions at once and bring down unlimited wonder into the world.

His heart raced as Donovan's bronze face came close to his. He was sure that as he kissed this boy and merged his dreams with his transitory lips, he would never again live among the gods. So he paused and watched the stars for some cautionary sign, but nothing came. Then he kissed him. As his lips parted Donovan's mouth, the gods of Salmacis saw their union and made the incarnation complete.

Jacobi finally sat calmly beside me; his head rested on my shoulder. Thinking of all he said, his intentions, and his nostalgic yearnings, a fragmented image passed before my mind's eye of something I had heard a long time ago. My tongue thrust against my teeth, trying to form the words. My throat contracted, but no sound came, and that which I had almost recollected was lost.

Who knows what intimacies our eyes may shout,
What evident secrets daily foreheads flaunt,
What panes of glass conceal our beating hearts?

Betrayal, by Emily Dickinson

Chapter Seven

Just as the height of interest about Jacobi reached a fever pitch, his mansion stayed dark one Saturday night—and, as mysteriously as it had begun, his gig as Charles Ponzi was up. Slowly, I noticed the sports cars and limousines that raced down his driveway pause and then drive sluggishly away. I was concerned he was sick, so I went over to check on him. A butler that I had never seen before—an ice block of a man with a mugshot for a face—peered at me from behind the door.

"Is Mr. Jacobi in?"

"Yep."

"Is he all right?"

"Uh-huh."

"I haven't seen him lately, and I'm a little worried. Please tell him Carry came to see him."

"Who are you to him?" he asked.

"Carry Iverson. A friend."

"Iverson. Yeah, I'll let him know."

He slammed the door.

The chatter around Emerald Bluff was that he had fired every one of his staff last week and then hired six new ones whom he made sign nondisclosure agreements and forbade them to leave the grounds. Everything was ordered in; trucks from new suppliers came and went. The drivers put the word out that the mansion had deteriorated into a slum. People suggested the new "staff" weren't really such but bodyguards.

The day after my visit Jacobi called me.

"Are you going on a trip?" I asked.

"No, mate."

"Rumor has it you fired all of your staff."

"I needed new people. People who wouldn't spread rumors. I see Donovan nearly every afternoon. It's for his protection."

So the whole harem collapsed onto itself under the weight of Donovan's judgment.

"Rosenberg sent them," said Jacobi. They had done something for him, so he wanted to repay them. They're all related and in the same business."

"Oh, really? The same *business*." I said. "Oskar, you sound depressed."

"Very much so. Donovan told me today he just wanted to run away with me. I tried to make him see it wouldn't work that way, and I just made things worse."

"So wait a minute. He wants you, and now you don't want him?"

"No. I mean yes I do. But we can't just run off. If we don't do this the right way, we'll both have demons lurking in every shadow."

"Maybe his way isn't dramatic enough for you."

"You're wrong," he talked over me. "He just needs to tell Fallon that he only loves me. Then we can go back to Columbus and start again. Let's drop this, mate. The reason I'm calling is because of Donovan. He wants you to come to lunch tomorrow at his house."

"I don't know. I—"

"Levi will be there," Jacobi said.

"Why are you dangling a carrot? And why couldn't—hold on, Donovan's calling now."

When I agreed to come to lunch, the tension in Donovan's voice melted. Something was going down. I feared Jacobi was going to use this opportunity to force fate to give him what he was owed.

A blazing heatwave settled into Austin on this last day of summer. I hovered over the seat in my SUV and tried to avoid any metal. I drove to the market to pick up a few bottles of wine before I made my way to Donovan's. As I got out of my car—the air conditioner had only begun to cool the air—the pre-lunch hustle and bustle broke me out of my daze. I opened the door to the market, and an arctic wind took my breath away. I stood in front of the beer and wine coolers with the door open long enough to stop the sweating. The wine I had wanted was sold out, so I settled for what they had. The woman standing in front of me at the cashier was fanning herself with a book. Her credit card smacked onto the floor.

"Goddammit," she yelled.

I scooped it up and made a show of not looking at the numbers, but she glared at me with suspicion.

"Fuckin' hot," said the cashier, a leathery soul with a long white beard in multicolored beads (except for the nicotine stains around his mustache). His straw hat tilted to one side. "What a damn hot summer!...Fuckin' hot!...Hot enough for you, boy?"

He slid the sticky-stained receipt across the counter. I was too hot to care why it was sticky, what he had touched, and who he did it with. But a few ideas floated through my mind.

Jacobi and I arrived together. We rang the bell and waited. I could almost make out what the butler was saying on the phone.

"Mrs. Macandeior's body?" I imagined him asking. "You can't have it today; it's far too hot to touch."

What he really said was, "Yes, of course. I'll check."

He opened the door to let us in, wiping beads of sweat from his forehead.

"Please, join the rest in the living room," he said, gesturing with an open palm—this extra effort on such a hot day made no sense.

The air conditioner pumped air through the Macandeior's house, but Fallon insisted on not making it too cold. Donovan and Levi slumped together on the sectional, fans on high, sprawled out like sultans holding on to their turbans in a strong wind.

"I'm melting..." said Levi. He took my hand and kissed it.

"And where is Mrs. Macandeior, the equestrian?" I asked.

"I heard that, Iverson," she yelled from the hall.

Jacobi stood on a hoary throw rug in the middle of the room. He looked around, captivated. Donovan watched him and chuckled.

"So, queens here's the low-down. We think that's Fallon's down-low on the phone," said Levi.

We became still and quiet. Fallon's voice rose: "Fine. Then the deal is off. I don't owe you anything. And fuck you for bothering me about it during lunch."

"Betcha there's no one on the phone at all," said Donovan.

"Yes, there is. I could hear the woman yelling," I said.

Fallon stomped into the room.

"Mr. Jacobi!" She put out her thin, spider-leg fingers and covered Jacobi's hand with her other palm, dominance asserted. "So nice to have you over, sir. And you, Carry," she said with a nod.

"Baby, make us a drink," Donovan said, feigning a whine.

When Fallon left the room, he jumped off the sofa and pulled Jacobi's face in for a kiss.

"I love you, Oskar Jacobi," he said.

"Not in front of the child," said Levi, indicating me.

Donovan looked at Levi.

"Come kiss Carry."

"I'm a vestal virgin. Shame on you, slut."

"The only thing vestal about you is your vagina. Now come kiss him!"

He went to pull Levi off the sectional but sat on his lap instead, deciding it was too hot to expend the energy. Just then, a clean-cut nanny carried a little boy into the room.

"My son in whom I'm well pleased," Donovan said, taking the toddler into his arms.

"Come to Daddy."

He propped the child on his knee like a ventriloquist's doll, and then placed his hand behind the boy's neck.

"Hello, everyone. Let's shake hands," Donovan said out of the corner of his mouth.

Jacobi and I took turns talking with the child. But all the while, Jacobi was riveted, as though he never believed the boy was real.

"Isn't he gorgeous?" asked Donovan. "We had this Versace tracksuit made especially for him, for special occasions."

The child pointed to Levi.

"That's right, Guncle Levi has on a pretty shirt, too."

"What do you think of daddy's friends?" Donovan turned the boy in Jacobi's direction. "Aren't they handsome?"

Donovan raised the drooling child in the air and handed him back to the nanny who carried him out of the room just as Fallon returned with four old-fashioned cocktails clinking with ice.

"He doesn't look like me," said Donovan. "He has Fallon's silky hair and pointy face." Donovan raised his drink. "To cold whiskey," he added.

"L'Chaim," said Jacobi awkwardly.

We sipped at first, and then the heat got the best of our manners, and we gulped them down.

"These dog days should teach those conservatives a lesson. If a summer like this doesn't convince them of global warming, they can go to hell," said Fallon. "Mr. Jacobi, walk with me outside."

I went with them. On the flashing blue Colorado, in the stale swelter, two small sailboats crossed paths. Jacobi watched them and then pointed across the river.

"I'm directly across from you."

"I'm aware," said Fallon.

Our eyes glanced across the garden and over the hot, dry rocks on the shore. The graceful white fin of another boat cut across the cerulean sky. Farther on were the cedars and oaks and simpler houses dotting the shore of Emerald Bluff.

"He's got the right idea," said Fallon, nodding toward the boat. "I'd like to be with him right now."

We ate lunch in the dining room: salads on chilled plates, fresh trout, green bean almondine, lemon meringue pie, and too much cold beer.

"I'm bored," said Donovan, tossing his fork onto the plate. "What's the plan for the day? And for tomorrow? And the next decade?"

"Chill, queen. You're taking the mellow out of dramatic," said Levi.

"It's so damn hot, though." Donovan guzzled the rest of his beer. "Let's go to Austin."

The frantic fanning of his hands pushed against the hot, humid air, sending it around the table to visit us like a moist specter.

"What do you think of my stables, Mr. Jacobi? I think I'm the only one around here who has air-conditioned horses."

"They're very impressive. I've seen similar stables in—"

"I'm going to Austin. Who's going with me?" asked Donovan. Jacobi's eyes locked with his. "Oskar, you are always so modish." Jacobi forced his eyes down at the table. "I know some hip shopping spots. Interested?"

He had told Jacobi he loved him, not caring if Fallon heard. But now she saw it. She was dumbstruck. Her lips trembled as she watched Jacobi, and then her mouth worked its way open into a snarl when she shifted her attention to Donovan.

"You remind me of that actor," Donovan went on. "Pine. What's his first—"

"Enough already," Fallon said. "I'll go to Austin. We're all going."

She got up. Her niobium eyes darted between Jacobi and her husband. We sat still as though embalmed.

"Get up," she yelled. "What are you waiting for? We're going to fucking Austin."

She took one last sip of her beer and set the glass on the table. Donovan stood first, and then the rest of us moved out to the blazing pavement.

"Wait," Donovan said. "I can't just go like this," he lifted his pants at the sides.

"You changed before lunch," said Fallon.

"That was hours ago, babe. And I'm drenched. It's too hot for cotton anyway."

Fallon lit a cigarette and sulked at him through the smoke.

"Batty boy's gotta point." Levi took Donovan's hand.

They went upstairs for a wardrobe change while we smoked. That severe luminary was already scorching the western sky. Jacobi opened his mouth as if to say something but cleared his throat instead. Fallon snapped a hand to her hip and waited.

"At least the horses are cool," said Jacobi.

"Why the hell are we going to Austin?" Fallon asked. "Those twats get an idea in their heads and—"

"Are we bringing liquor?" yelled Donovan from an upstairs window.

"I'll get the Macallan," said Fallon and went inside.

Jacobi's face was red.

"I can't do this here, mate."

"I get it. Donovan can't keep his voice down," I said. "He sounds like—"

"He sounds like gold," he said.

And there it was, the thing that had eluded me about Jacobi. Donovan's mellifluous voice was like gold—it was free and easy, enchanting, the shine in it, the weight of it…The king's son locked in a tower…saved by Rumpelstiltskin…

Fallon came back outside with the whiskey in a large shopping bag, and then Donovan and Levi trotted out wearing pinstriped suits and fedoras.

"Let's take my car," said Jacobi. He leaned against it but then moved away. "It's hot. I should have parked in the shade."

"Looks like it's manual," said Fallon.

"It is."

"You drive my car. I want to take yours for a spin."

Jacobi frowned. "It's low on gas."

"It's fine. We're not driving cross country. Besides, there are plenty of gas stations on the way."

We all froze again, except for Fallon, who held her hand out for the fob. Donovan shook his head at Fallon as if she'd suggested they trade permanently. An expression rippled across Jacobi's face.

"Get in, Donovan," said Fallon, shoving him toward Jacobi's car. "This is going to be a ride you'll never forget."

Donovan resisted. "You drive Carry and Levi. Oskar and I will follow."

He stood next to Jacobi, brushing his hand with his finger. I crawled in the back, and Levi and Fallon sat up front. Fallon revved the engine, and we roared away with the top down.

"I see what's going on," said Fallon, looking at me in the rearview mirror.

"What's going on?" I asked.

"Iverson, don't fuck with me. I see things other people can't or won't. And not just with my eyes. I have a spot-on instinct. Don't you remember at Oberlin when you—"

I don't know what made her stop midsentence, but I was relieved she did.

"I've had a friend look into him," she said.

"You mean that butler who reads the cards?" asked Levi.

"What in the hell are you talking about?" Fallon gave us the finger as we laughed. "Cards?"

"Yeah, the tarot kind, hon."

"No, I had a PI friend comb through his past."

"And what? You found a picture of him in a Harvard hoodie?" joked Levi.

"Harvard! Like hell. The man wears fur coats."

"He's still a Harvard man...*fur real*." Levi slapped the dash. "And if you think he's so sus, why did you invite him to lunch?" asked Levi.

"It was Donovan. You know they knew each other *before* we got married? Who knows what dump they met in."

We were all pissed now with the hot air and the escalating sobriety, which kept us quiet for a while. Then the Giantess came into view as we took the loop onto the road along Lady Bird Lake. Fallon kept glancing in the rearview mirror.

"I have to make a pit stop."

"See? Jacobi said there wasn't enough gas," Levi said.

"There's plenty of fucking gas."

Fallon took a sharp turn and stopped at Shyla Kearns' salon. She honked until the woman tottered out.

"What took you so long?"

"I'm having a rough day," said Shyla.

"I bet you are. But not so rough you had to call me during lunch."

"I'm sorry, but I desperately need that money for a car. No car, no second job."

"Poor dear. But how do you like my new car?" asked Fallon. "I just bought it."

"I like that color," said Shyla.

"I'll sell it to you."

"Yeah, right. I could buy a house before I could get a car like that," Shyla said, her face seeming to age as the smile left it.

"What do you need a second job for? I warned you about the salon and—"

"My husband and I want to save up and move to Florida."

"Your husband," said Fallon. She removed her sunglasses.

"He's been showing me pictures of places we could rent. He talks about it all the time."

Jacobi and Donovan raced by us, kicking up loose gravel.

"I learned something questionable a couple of days ago, Mrs. Macandeior, and we just need to get out. That's why I need that other job."

My mouth was dry, and I had a headache. The air vents were pointed directly at Fallon and Levi, and none of the cold air was reaching me. I wondered if Shyla suspected Fallon, but the way she was asking for a loan made me reconsider; she was having a rough day because she discovered that Liam had a life outside of their world together. I looked at Shyla, then at Fallon, who just had the same epiphany an hour ago—and I realized then that the most significant difference between people wasn't race, gender, or sexuality. It was between those who were fulfilled and those who weren't.

"I'll send the money over to you tomorrow," said Fallon.

This part of Austin always made me look over my shoulder, even in broad daylight, and as I did, I saw the edges of the Giantess's hotel and the tattered gray tents of the homeless camps. When I turned back toward the salon, I saw a figure in the window.

Liam Kearns was watching his wife and Fallon so keenly he was not aware of my stare. Anger, betrayal, and pain flickered across his face in succession, as though it were a slide show projection screen. I'd seen those emotions cross over faces looking back at me, but on Liam Kearns' they seemed out of place until I studied his eyes which brimmed with jealousy, and presently glared at Levi who Liam assumed was Fallon's husband.

* * *

There is no hobgoblin like uncertainty, and as we sped away, Fallon was in a panic. Her husband and her paramour, until now, had been anchored to the port of security. Now the rope had snapped, and her life was drifting out of control. Frenzied, she drove faster, intending to pass Donovan and to put distance between her and Liam. We bolted uptown twenty miles over the speed limit until we were close to the leisurely blue car.

"That restored theatre on Congress is fabulous," said Levi. "I love Austin in the afternoon. There's something sexy about it. It's like waking up from a nap after a good fuck."

"Sexy" made Fallon's face twitch. The blue car stopped at a light, and Donovan waved his hand for Fallon to pull up next to them.

"Where from here, babe?" he asked.

"Levi wants to go to a fucking movie."

"It'll be too crowded with this heat," he said. "You take the boys to a movie, and we'll meet you later. Just look for me in drag on some corner."

The driver behind us leaned into his horn. "That's no good," Fallon said. "Follow me to the Archer Hotel."

She drove slower now, checking the rearview mirror for their car, slowing down further if she lost sight of them for a moment. I suspect she was worried they would hop on the interstate and leave her behind forever.

But we all arrived at the Archer together and made the ridiculous choice to book the king suite with a fireplace and a balcony.

I've forgotten the details of the argument that embarrassed us all in the lobby, but I have an intense muscle memory of my boxers wedged in my ass as if they were running from a pair of scissors. It all started with Donovan suggesting we book five different rooms so that we each could take our own cold showers. Then the scheme evolved into something more realistic; we just needed a place to enjoy the Macallan. We all argued about the farcical notion of five rooms against the merits of one large room. We involved the front desk receptionist, talking over each other at him to help us resolve our debate. We thought we were hilarious, but the receptionist's hands perched over the keyboard, and he stared at us with an open mouth. Other guests had become impatient and offered their suggestions, some of which were quite vulgar.

The outrageously large suite was posh, but the air had been turned off, and it was stuffy. Even though it was already four o'clock, the hot clime outside compelled us to turn on the air conditioner and lower the thermostat immediately. Donovan closed the curtains and turned on a couple of lights.

"Thank God for the fireplace. Is someone going to light it up?" jeered Levi, and everyone laughed or pretended to laugh.

"Can someone turn the fan higher?" asked Donovan.

"It's as high as it will go."

"Then let's call down for buckets of ice, for the tub."

"There is no tub," said Fallon. "It's a walk-in shower. So let the air conditioner work and quit bitching about the heat."

She took the Macallan out of the shopping bag and set it on a table.

"Don't you think you're being harsh?" asked Jacobi. "You decided we would all come here."

No one spoke or made eye contact. The welcome booklet slid off a shelf, landed with a thud, and opened in the middle. Levi said, "This place better not be haunted," but no one laughed.

"Here, let me," I said.

"No worries, mate," said Jacobi lifting it from the floor. He leafed through the pages and then pointed to some item on one of them. "Well, look at that."

"That's your go-to word, isn't it?" Fallon said.

"Which word?"

"'Mate' this and 'mate' that. Where did you learn that from? Not in the Midwest and probably not at *Harvard*."

"Christ, Fallon," said Donovan, wiping the back of his sweaty neck. "If you're just going to make us more miserable, you can leave. Otherwise, pour us some whiskey."

Fallon lined up five glasses in a sharp row. Levi paired his phone to the Bowers & Wilkins Zeppelin speakers, and soon we were listening to a man telling his mama he liked boys.

"Imagine schtupping anyone in this heat," yelled Levi over the music.

"I remember sneaking out of the house during one of the hottest nights of the summer," said Donovan. "Who was I going to meet? Oh, that's right, Levi!"

"And what were we going to do, bitch?"

"I'm sure everyone here would like to know." Donovan pressed his finger to his lips as Fallon's back was turned. "But let's keep that to ourselves."

"Which part?" asked Levi. "The cock warts or how that guy's ass—"

"What was the name of that boy?" asked Donovan.

"Chad the Chode," answered Levi.

"Chad. And he was from Chattanooga."

"And we had to take him to the hospital," said Levi. "Because we were just blocks from the Ohio State ER. It seemed like he was there forever, but I remember the day he got out, my father died." He changed the song. "They were unrelated events."

"I wonder what he's doing now," Donovan said.

"He's an endocrinologist in Chicago. I only know because some friends up there use him."

"Who?" asked Donovan.

"Jamie was his most recent."

"Recent what?" I asked.

"Gender confirmation."

"Sex change. Just call it what it is," said Fallon.

"I just did. And don't start in on all that political bullshit, Fallon. Anyway, Chad graduated from Stanford. We need more people like that."

"We're old," said Donovan. "If we could turn the clock back ten years, we would be dancing."

"Yeah, but to very different music," Levi looked at Fallon.

Jacobi bounced his heel against the floor out of rhythm with the music.

Fallon flashed her eyes at him. "I hear you're a Harvard man, Mr. Jacobi."

"Not quite."

"Of course, you are. You attended Harvard, as I've heard."

"I went there."

"And when exactly were you there? I wonder if you might know any of my friends."

A waiter knocked on the door and brought in complimentary hors d'oeuvres and wine, but the silence only solidified as he pulled the door closed. Fallon was determined to check this item off of her list.

"I said I went there," said Jacobi.

"I'm not deaf, but I want to know when."

"It was around two-thousand and five. I was only there a few months. That's why I don't call myself a Harvard man."

Fallon turned around, hoping to find doubt on our faces. We all looked at Jacobi.

"I was just giving it a try," he said. "I could have gone anywhere but—" and then he lost his momentum.

I wanted to get up and put my arm around him. His candor revived that confidence in him I'd felt before.

Donovan crossed the room and took hold of Fallon's elbow. "Finish pouring the whiskey and give yourself a double. Then you won't feel so thick."

"Take your hand off me," growled Fallon. "I have another question for Mr. Jacobi."

"Which is?" asked Jacobi, leaning toward her with genuine curiosity.

"Why are you trying to fuck up my marriage?"

They had finally come out of the closet. The tension in Jacobi's face melted, and his shoulders dropped.

"He's not fucking anything up," said Donovan, pointing a finger in Fallon's face. "You're the dirty bird shitting in your own nest."

"I'm the one shitting," repeated Fallon. "I guess you'd think the hip thing for me to do would be to let Mr. Loser from Cuntville fuck my husband. Well, I'm not the *menage a trois* type. Next, you'll be asking for an open marriage so we can gangbang Levi and Carry along with him."

"Carry's already fucking me," added Levi.

Everyone turned to me for a moment.

"Well, technically—" I started.

"Oh, now what? You can't consider yourself a 'Harvard man' either?" said Levi with a grin.

Fallon ignored him. "I have given you everything, Donovan. Not parties, not a grotesque mansion on Emerald Bluff. But the status, and all the money you could ever want, and the richest, modern home. And a son! Can *he* give you a son?"

I was hurting for Donovan but that she threw their son in last on the list almost made me laugh.

"Now I have something to say to you, mate," said Jacobi. Donovan intuited what was coming.

"Please don't!" he said. "Let's go home. Let's drop everything and leave."

I stood up. "Brilliant idea. Forget the whiskey, Fallon. No one's in the mood for a drink now."

"I want to hear what Mr. Jacobi has to say."

"Your husband doesn't love you," said Jacobi. "He's only ever loved me."

"You must have a mental health condition," said Fallon.

Jacobi leaped to his feet with violence in his eyes.

"He's only loved me. Do you understand that?" he yelled. "He married you because I was a zero, that's true. And because he was exhausted from hiding who he really is for so long. But he belongs to me."

Levi had stood up now, and we tried to leave, but Fallon and Jacobi stopped us both, as though they each had liberated themselves from the constraints of propriety, and all that mattered was for us to witness their fury, like the spectators in Rome.

"Donovan, sit." Her tone then changed to her business voice. "Help me understand here. Tell me everything."

"I've already told you," said Jacobi. "For the last five years, our love has survived."

Fallon whipped her head toward Donovan.

"You've been fucking him for the last five years?"

"Not like that. We never saw each other in person. But we've loved each other since we met, mate, and you were the last to figure it out. I pitied you," but there was no pity now, "when I thought about how certain you were of your life."

"Oh—well, I thought this was serious." Fallon sat in the chair and examined her nails. "You've lost your mind, Jacobi.

That's what's pitiful. I don't care about five years ago. Hell, I didn't even know Donovan then. And it's pathetic how you've maneuvered back into his life, building that garish thing across the river hoping he would want you again. But you're a liar. Donovan loved me the day we got married, and he would do it all over again."

"You're wrong," Jacobi said.

"No, you're just a fool who can't see past your own delusions. You don't know him like I do. He gets these longings that clutter up his mind, but they don't mean anything." She pressed her palms together as if in mediation. "And I love him. More than you ever could. I've made mistakes, but my love has never wavered."

"You're a horse-faced bitch," said Donovan to her. And then to me: "Do you know why we lived like vagabonds in Europe? It's a wonder no one has told you by now."

Jacobi walked over and stood next to Donovan.

"It's in the past. None of it matters now. Just tell her I'm the only one you've ever loved—and then the slate will be wiped clean."

Donovan looked at Jacobi, as if through cataracts. "What's the point? How could I have ever loved her?"

"Exactly. You never did. Now tell her."

Jacobi waited, but Donovan only looked at Levi and me searching for a way out, as though he realized what he had said—and as though he had never wanted to say it at all. But the damage had been done.

"I never loved her," he said and averted his eyes from Fallon.

"Not in Trastevere?" asked Fallon sternly.

"No."

The speakers billowed out smokey chords that drifted in the warmth of the room.

"And not on the day when we ran through the lavender fields in Provence?" Fallon's voice withered. "Donovan?"

"Please, stop." His face was harsh, but there was no bitterness in his voice. He looked at Jacobi. "Now I've said it, Oskar." His hand shook as he tried to light a cigarette. Frustrated, he threw it across the room, where it landed on the bed.

"You demand so much," he yelled at Jacobi. "You know I love you—why put me through all of this? I can't choose between what we had and what I have with her." He was crying now. "I love you both."

Jacobi's eyes widened.

"Both?" he echoed.

"I call bullshit on that one, too," said Fallon. "You were dead to him. Donovan and I have a bond you'll never understand and can never have."

Jacobi flinched as if her words had bitten him.

"I'm going to talk to my husband alone. He's having one of his episodes now—"

"It won't change a thing whether we're alone or here. I can't say I never loved Fallon."

"See?" agreed Fallon.

He turned to his wife.

"Not that my love means anything to you," he said.

"It means everything to me now. We'll be better."

"I'm afraid you've misunderstood," said Jacobi unnerved. "You've lost your chance to be better."

"Oh, have I?" her laugh heckled Jacobi. She had the currency now to deal in certainty. "And why the fuck is that?"

"Donovan is divorcing you."

"No, he isn't."

"I—I am, Fallon," he said, visibly afraid.

"He's not going anywhere," Fallon's voice roared down onto Jacobi. "And not for a fuckwad drug dealer who would trade his mother's soul for the ring to put on his finger."

"I can't take it. Please, let's leave," screamed Donovan.

"Who do you think you are, anyway?" hissed Fallon. "You're one of Gabriel Rosenberg's cronies, aren't you? I know all about him and your dealings with Rosenberg. And you can count on me destroying you with what I know."

"Be my guest," said Jacobi, voice resolute.

"I know all about your big pharma deals." She turned to us and spoke rapid-fire. "Jacobi and Rosenberg bought billions of stock in pharmaceutical companies around the world and leveraged the companies to make the drugs more addicting. And that's just the beginning of his sick side hustles. Wait until you hear about the rent bo—"

"What about your own double dealings? Your man Alex Morgan was more than happy to get in on a deal—as your proxy."

"And because you fucked him over, he's in federal prison. You should hear my little bird sing about you now," Fallon said.

"You sent him to us because you were greedy. And I don't remember you complaining about the returns you garnered, *mate*."

"I'm not your 'mate'!" snapped Fallon. Jacobi smirked. "Morgan and I could've shut you down over the inside trading, but Rosenberg scared the shit out of him."

Jacobi's eyes narrowed, his upper lipped trembled.

"And the pharmaceuticals are not the only income stream for you," said Fallon, her words measured and paced. "You've got another scheme going that Morgan is disinclined to tell me about."

Donovan glowered at Jacobi and Fallon. Then he looked at Levi who was playing a game on his phone. When I glanced back at Jacobi, I was dismayed at the appearance of his face. He looked—and I hate to repeat the slander uttered in his garden—like he could "kill a man." I wish there were another description, but the set of his jaw and the rage in his eyes fit it perfectly.

As soon as he started to speak to Donovan, the look was gone.

"Donovan, please, don't believe a word Fallon has said. You know me. You know my character. I'm not a fraud, and I don't have illegal businesses."

With every counterexample and plea, Donovan sank deeper into himself.

"I don't employ sex workers. I'm not involved in human trafficking." He continued to deny allegations that Fallon never even brought up. But Donovan put his hands to his ears and rocked himself as though he were a fragile child. Seeing this, Jacobi dropped his defense, leaving his dream to bleed out, gurgle, and cling to life as the sun was finishing its work for the day.

The silence was interrupted by a whimper—a voice begging.

"Dammit, Fallon. This is killing me. Can we please leave?"

Donovan's dead eyes betrayed his brokenness, and the fortitude he had possessed to give Jacobi everything was gone.

"You and Jacobi go home," said Fallon. "In Jacobi's car."

"I should ride with you," Donovan protested.

"It's for your own damn good. Jacobi's little schoolboy fantasy is over. Now you can watch him wallow."

They left without saying goodbye as if vaporized, not leaving a trace for me to offer compassion.

Fallon put the whiskey back in the bag. "You boys want this?"

I couldn't answer.

"Carry?" Fallon asked me directly.

"I'm sorry, what?"

"Do. You. Want. This?"

"I can't believe I forgot," I said.

"Forgot what?" asked Levi.

"Today is my birthday."

I was twenty-five. I felt the next twenty-five years looming over me, dark and dangerous.

Fallon left us to make a phone call. Levi moved to the bed. "Come here, Carry."

He pulled me close to him and molded his body against mine, removing the pang of empty space and satiating my skin-hunger.

"Don't take all this so hard. It will pass." Levi turned my face toward his parted lips and pressed them against my cheek. He sucked at my chin and neck, and then let his tongue relish its way down my chest and waist. Afterward, our faces were pulpy from lust.

Around seven o'clock, we got into Fallon's car and started out to Lake Travis. Fallon talked like she was on a stimulant, shouting and laughing. Levi and I were as deaf to her racket as the boisterous crowds on the sidewalk or the rumbling of the road beneath us.

One can only commiserate so much. Levi and I had crossed that threshold and were numb, letting their drama fade to the background. Twenty-five—the impending fate of loneliness, a thinning list of men to know, a shallow glass of fervor, a body no one will want to look at or touch. But Levi, unlike Donovan and Oskar, was too shrewd to drag the deadweight of dreams and hope from the past to the future. As we passed downtown, his amber face rested indolently against my shoulder, and the blaring alarm of twenty-five was turned off with the heat of his palm on my leg.

So we drove on toward destruction in the fresh cool air of the lavender night.

* * *

From a distance away, we saw several cars and a crowd.

"Shit," said Fallon. "There's been an accident. Now we're blocked."

She slowed down, still complaining, but as we approached, the clamoring of the paramedics and the concern on people's faces made her quiet.

"Might as well take a look," she said.

When we opened our doors, I heard a sorrowful howl coming from near the salon, a sound which, as we got out of the car, rendered into words: "Oh, my God! No, God, please!" over and over in an inexhaustible moan.

"This looks really bad," said Fallon eagerly.

She shoved past a circle of people and looked toward the building which was lit by a single orange street light. Then she let out a sharp sound, and with a frantic striking motion with her thin hands, she made her way to the ambulance.

The circle re-formed as new onlookers were absorbed, and they inched loser as running commentary passed along the group. In the reconstruction of the circle, Levi and I found ourselves closer to the scene.

Liam Kearns' body, covered in a sheet, lay on a gurney near the ambulance, and Fallon was bending over it, frozen. Next to her stood a police officer getting names and correcting notes as sweat ran down her face. I looked around to find the moaning words that echoed across the surrounding buildings—then I saw Shyla standing on the sidewalk, knees shaking, holding on to a fencepost. A man talked to her, trying to comfort her, laying a kind hand on her shoulder, but Shyla didn't see or hear him. She looked at the streetlight as if in prayer and then back to the body, and then jumped back to the light again, and wailed: "Oh, God, no! Oh, my Lord. Oh, Jesus, please, no!"

Fallon's eyes darted around the street and salon and then locked on the police officer. She mumbled something to her.

"A-b-u-n-n," the police officer said, "—d—"

"One n—" corrected the man, "A-b-u-n-d-i-o—"

"Hey, I'm talking to you," said Fallon.

"d—" said the officer, "i—"

"o—"

"o—" She looked up when Fallon slapped her hand on her shoulder. "Remove your hand, ma'am."

"I want to know what happened."

The officer looked at the body. "A car hit him. He didn't stand a chance."

"Hit him?" repeated Fallon.

"He ran out into the street. Probably a hit and run. The guy didn't even stop."

"Sorry, but there were two cars," said Abundio, "one coming and one going."

"Where were they headed, sir?" asked the officer.

"How do I know?"

"What direction, sir?" the officer clarified.

"One was going each way. And this man," he nearly touched the body, but his hand stopped midway and dropped to his side, "he ran out, and the one coming from downtown drove right over him. I figure they were going at least fifty."

"What's the name of this business?" asked the officer.

"It doesn't have a name."

A man in a suit stood beside Fallon.

"The car was yellow," he said, "a fancy sports car."

"Did you see the accident, sir?" asked the officer.

"I didn't. But the car sped past me down the street. He had to be going sixty miles an hour."

"Let me get your name and contact information."

Shyla must have heard some of this conversation. She was still holding onto the fence, but there was a new variation in her groaning dirge:

"I know that car. And I know who drives it. Lord help me, I know."

Fallon's shoulders rode up her neck and she clenched her teeth. She darted over to Shyla and grabbed her arms.

"You get yourself together," she said, trying to sound calm.

Shyla looked at Fallon; she started to raise her fist but nearly collapsed. Fallon held onto her, shaking her body. "Clear your head. I just pulled up a few minutes ago from downtown. I was driving that blue car to deliver it to you, to ease the financial burden, you understand? That yellow car I was driving this afternoon wasn't mine. I just said it to—I lied, all right? I haven't been in it all afternoon."

The man in the suit and I were close enough to hear what she said, but something in her tone got the attention of the police officer. She looked over at them wide-eyed and head tilted.

"What's going on over there?" she asked.

"I'm her friend." Fallon met the officer's eyes but held Shyla's arms. "She says she's familiar with the car that killed—that caused the accident. It was yellow."

The sharp-witted officer focused her gaze on Fallon.

"And what color is your car?"

"It's blue. That one over there."

"We were coming from downtown," I said.

Someone who had been driving behind us told the officer it was true, and she turned to another witness.

"Would you please spell your name again for me?"

Fallon put her arm around Shyla and walked her back to the salon, set her in a chair, and came back.

"Would one of you rubberneckers go sit with her?" she demanded. She watched the two men closest to her, suggesting the other one should help, but the two finally opted to go together. Fallon made her way to me, avoiding the gurney. She whispered: "It's time to leave."

Without making a commotion, she weaved in and out of the crowd, and we followed. The coroner arrived as we were leaving.

Fallon drove under the speed limit until we passed the bell tower and onto the freeway. Then she hammered the gas pedal, and the blue car bolted past the dark trees and rocky hills along the route to The Hollows. I heard a gravelly whimper and saw tears flowing down her face.

"The fucking pussy!" she yelled. "Didn't even stop."

* * *

The Macandeior's house emerged through the gnarly trees. Fallon parked beside the porch and looked up to the second floor, where two windows glowed through billowing curtains.

"Donovan's here," she said. We got out of the car, and she looked at me. "I should have taken you to your house, Carry. There's nothing you can do for us tonight."

The indifference and arrogance that always accompanied Fallon were no longer present. She was decisive and serious, as though she were inhabited by a spirit conjured up by a benevolent necromancer. We stood on the moonlit porch. I felt stranded, but Fallon soon fixed everything, the way a mother soothes a skinned knee.

"I'll call you an Uber. While you wait, you and Levi should have something to eat—if you can."

"No thanks, but I would appreciate you getting that Uber. I'll wait outside."

Levi put his hand on my shoulder.

"Carry, come in."

"No, it's not a good idea."

My stomach was churning. I needed to be alone. But Levi kissed my neck and glided his lips to my ear.

"It's only nine-thirty," he said.

There was no way in hell I was going in; I was over all of them after today, and when I looked at Levi, I was disgusted with him too. He pulled back and scanned my face. He must have seen it because he dropped his arm from my shoulder and twisted his body around and hurried up the steps into the house. I sat down and ran my fingers through my hair, wanting to pull just hard enough to make my scalp ache. The butler stepped out of the front door to inform me the driver was on the way. Then I meandered down the driveway away from the house, away from the gloom, away from them.

I hadn't but reached the gate when I heard my name. Jacobi walked out of the bushes. I must have stepped out of my body by then because I experienced everything as if from a camera angle just over my head. Dazed, I looked at Jacobi—or I saw myself see Jacobi—and could only focus on the radiance of his white suit spotlighted by the moon.

"What the hell are you doing in the bushes?" I asked.

"Just standing here, mate."

After all that had happened, "standing here" was a shameful decision. That murderous look had returned to his face, and for all I knew, he was lying in wait to kill Fallon. It wouldn't have surprised me at this point to discover that "Rosenberg's mob" was lurking behind him in the bushes.

"Did you see anything on your way here?" he asked.

"Yes."

His breath quickened, but he was silent for a moment.

"Is he dead?"

"Yes."

"I was afraid he was. I told Donovan he was dead. His dithering about it would only delay the shock. I tried to tell him he was dead. Donovan will be all right."

His focus was only on Donovan's feelings. Bitterness frothed from my bowels into my throat.

"I made it to Emerald Bluff using side roads," he told me. "And parked the car in my garage. I doubt anyone saw us, but I can't be sure."

I hated him. And there was no reason to tell him he was wrong.

"Who was the man?" he asked.

"Liam Kearns. His wife owns the salon. What happened, Oskar?"

"I tried to grab the wheel and swerve—" He paused and looked away from me, realizing I knew the truth.

"Donovan was driving," I said.

"Yes, but no one can know that, Carry. I'm going to say it was me. He was so shaken when we left Austin, and he thought driving would settle his mind—then this man ran out into the street as we were passing an oncoming car. It happened in seconds, but I remember him looking at us like he wanted to say something like he knew us. So Donovan veered away from him toward the oncoming car and then panicked and steered right at him—I think he died on impact."

"He was torn open—"

"Stop. I don't want to picture it, mate." He wiped his eyes. "After, Donovan hit the gas. I told him to stop, but he was in a fugue, so I pulled the emergency brake. He collapsed into my lap, and I drove us home."

"He's going to be fine. He'll get himself together tomorrow," he said, looking at the illuminated windows upstairs. "I'll wait here and see if Fallon causes a scene about what happened this afternoon. He's locked himself in that room, and if Fallon starts in, he's going to signal me by flashing the light."

"She's not going to hurt him," I said. "She has more to worry about than Donovan."

"I don't trust her, mate. She's volatile."

"So, how long are you going to stalk them in the bushes?"

"All night if I have to. At least until they go to sleep."

A thought occurred to me that shifted my perspective. What if Fallon found out that Donovan was driving Jacobi's car? She might leverage that—she could do anything with it.

I looked at the house. A few windows were lit up now downstairs, and the yellow glow from Donovan's room illuminated the landscaping beneath it.

"Stay here," I said. "I'll go see what's going on."

I hurried along the border between the driveway and the lawn and snuck up the porch stairs. Through the glass windows, I could see the living room was empty. I crept across the patio where we had gathered that June night for dinner three months ago. There was a light on in the kitchen. The blinds were down, but I found a view through a gap at the bottom.

Donovan and Fallon were sitting across from each other at the kitchen table. A cold brisket was between them with two bottles of beer. Fallon was addressing him fervently with sharp gestures, and then, with her gentle gravity, she placed her hand on his, stroking it as she spoke. She never took her gaze off of him, and occasionally he nodded, affirming her point.

Their faces were rigid, and they moved mechanically when they picked at the brisket, but neither brought a bite of food to their mouths. The bottles of beer sat in a pool of condensation, untouched. And yet they talked in a rhythm, their postures mirrored each other, and they seemed to look into each other's eyes as if naked, vulnerable, and accepting. They were a living portrait of collaboration.

I heard the Uber pull up in the driveway. I tiptoed from the porch away from the house. Jacobi was still waiting in the bushes.

"Could you see anything?" He bit his lip. "What's going on?"

"Everything seems okay," I answered, trying to sound neutral. "Come with me. Go home and get some sleep, Oskar."

He waved his hand in the air.

"I'm waiting here until Donovan goes to bed. Go on home, mate."

He gave my shoulder a rub. I looked at his hand. His long, thin fingers worked at my muscle, and for a moment, I felt electric. "Sleep well, Carry. I'll be okay." Then he put his hands in his pocket and inspected the house. Lost in his vigil, he no longer saw me. I walked toward the car and left him standing there in a shadow, a place the moon could not touch so that he could keep watch over nothing.

* * *

The middle-aged Latino, Abundio, who owned the liquor store steps from the Giantess, was the main witness during the investigation. He had napped throughout the heat of the day until after five when he took a walk along the route to the salon. He saw Shyla Kearns stuffing trash bags in a bin, looking pale and unsteady.

"You should be in bed," said Abundio.

"I can't. Need to keep the shop open. We gotta have the business."

"Señora, you're in no shape to work. Please, lie down for a bit."

There was a loud crash coming from the salon. Then someone started yelling.

"My husband is in there trashing the place," said Shyla, shrugging her shoulders. "He's pissed over nothin'. We've been saving up to move, and now he's got different ideas."

Abundio was surprised; he had known the Kearns for four years and had never seen them argue. Shyla was always exhausted; when she wasn't working, she sat on a lawn chair with a beer and watched the people and cars and life go by. Liam was hard working. He seemed like a family man, constantly checking on his people in North Austin. Shyla ran the roost, but the two had worked out their own kind of love.

"He sounds furious, Señora. What will happen?"

Shyla wouldn't respond. She eyed Abundio with suspicion.

"Say, what were you doing last Sunday afternoon?" asked Shyla.

"I'm sorry. I don't remember."

"And what about the Saturday night before. You see anything?" she asked.

Abundio shifted his gaze over Shyla's shoulder. Customers were headed to his liquor store.

"I need to get back to the store," he said. "Maybe I'll see you later."

He never came back. He testified that he got busy and just forgot. But when he stepped out again, sometime after seven, he remembered their conversation because he heard Liam yelling again.

"Just walk all over me!" he heard him say. "Why don't you just throw me out and get on with your life!"

Seconds later, Liam ran out into the dark, shouting and waving his hands wildly—and before Abundio could step out of his store, the horror had happened.

The "murder car," as the news called it, didn't stop; it roared out of the black mass of darkness, veered carelessly, and then disappeared around the curve. Abundio said he wasn't sure about the color—he had told the police officer it was lime green. The other car, the one heading to Austin, stopped just past the accident and then reversed and stopped near Liam Kearns' body, where his life was brutally obliterated. The driver knelt in the street and tried to find Kearns' neck to check for a pulse.

Abundio and this man were the first on the scene, and when they had torn open his shirt, wet with sweat and blood, they saw his chest sliced open, exposing tissue, ribs, and organs. They knew there was nothing they could do. The mouth was opened as if frozen in a scream, but the jaw hung sideways, mouth ripped at the corners, as though he had violently protested letting go of his life.

My spirit, though, is cracked; when as she can
  She chants to fill the cool night's emptiness,
  Too often can her weakening voice be said
  To sound the rattle of a wounded man
  Beside a bloody pool, stacked with the dead,
  Who cannot budge, and dies in fierce distress!

"The Cracked Bell," by Charles Baudelaire

Chapter Eight

I tossed and turned all night; the boats on the lake clanged like endless church bells, and I couldn't sleep. Gory images and terrifying half-sleeping dreams haunted my mind. I heard a car turn into Jacobi's driveway near dawn, and I jumped out of bed to dress. I had to warn him about something now, for once morning came, it would be too late.

I jogged across his yard. His front door was open, and he was leaning against the jamb. His body slumped. The dark circles under his eyes were proof that he had not slept.

"He's okay," he said, voice thin and hoarse. "I waited until four o'clock when he came to the window and looked out at me. Then he turned out the light."

Jacobi's mansion had never seemed so cavernous as it did that late night as we searched for cigarettes in the large hall and through the numerous entertainment rooms and lounges. We opened drawers; we trailed our hands over countless feet of darkness for light switches—once, I crashed into him, causing him to fall on the piano keys, kicking up dust from the spectral instrument. We paused there in a sort of embrace. When he looked at my mouth, my lips parted against my will. I was relieved the dust made him sneeze, and I laughed, taking a step back. All the rooms were musty, not having been cleaned for days. I finally found a silver cigarette case on a table I'd never noticed. There were two stale cigarettes inside. We walked to the lounge, dangerously close to each other, and sat on a sofa. The orange glow of our cigarettes swelled and waned in the darkness.

"You need to get out of this place. Out of Austin," I said. "They're going to find out it was your car."

"Leave *now*, mate? Donovan needs—"

"Go to Las Vegas or The Keys for a month or two."

"I can't leave. Donovan might show up here at any time, ready to make our move."

"Oskar, look at this place. Look at you. He's not—"

Jacobi stopped me with his hand. There was no convincing him. He would rather molder away, waiting to see what Donovan would do than put this behind him. He was holding on to the last brittle shard of hope, and I didn't want to be the one to shatter it.

Dawn was coming. But before its light broke the fragile intimacy between us, Jacobi told me the bizarre story about his relationship with Morty Foster. I think he told me at that time because "Oskar Jacobi" had been dissolved like limestone in Fallon's acidic rancor, and his long-held secrets couldn't protect him anymore. His openness made me think that he would confess to anything I wanted to know, but Donovan was the only thing on his mind.

He was the first "worthy" boy Jacobi had ever known. He'd met similar men on his journeys with Foster, but there was always an impassable membrane between them. He was spellbound when he first met Donovan. He visited his house, at first with an entourage of young people already riding his coattails. After that, he went alone. Jacobi staggered at Donovan's family home—Foster had taken him to the homes of the wealthy—but what singled out this beautiful house, what took Jacobi's breath away, was only that Donovan lived there. There was a succulent mystique about it, decorous bedrooms out of reach to the casual guest, people of all ages discussing important things, some jibing and laughing with each other. There was passion thick in the air and alive like the fragrant water lotus thrusting upward, opening itself to suck in the sun. And there were the men pursuing Donovan—men who were in love with him—and I believe their desire elevated his value in Jacobi's eyes. He sensed their yearning throughout the house, saturating the air with the smell of ripe libido.

"The fact that I was able to get into Donovan's house was a fluke," said Jacobi. "I was scheming hard back then to set up a future for myself, but I had to figure out how to use my inheritance from Foster." He shook his head and smiled. "And in the beginning, I took a lot of missteps."

"Missteps?"

He put his arm around me and leaned close.

"I had no past. At least not one I wanted people to know about. The truth is my parents were poor. They were struggling, working-class people."

He lowered his eyes. But his openness, at last, endeared me.

"Sure. I had one suit that Foster bought me, but I'd outgrown it. So I bought the finest shirts and shoes, went to a tanning salon once a week, hired a personal trainer. I needed to look like I lived a life that someone would envy, or at least respect." He shook his head again and laughed. "But I knew nothing about investing or saving. It was Rosenberg who took me under his wing and taught me how to use my money to make more."

"But not by saving and investing," I added.

Jacobi shook his head.

I remembered Mr. Rosenberg speaking fondly about Jacobi at lunch. I was still puzzled over his comment about wishing he could take Jacobi home to his mother.

"Was he in love with you?" I asked.

"He was. For a while, he filled in the space Foster had left in my life. But when I met Donovan, that affair was over."

"But he continued to help you?"

"Of course. He protected me from the worst kind of people. I learned from him until I became too greedy."

"You hurt him, didn't you?"

"A few times. He finally turned me loose and watched as I took whatever I could get from people. And eventually, I was in a position to take Donovan, all the while having no right to even be in his presence."

Had I been in his shoes, I would have hated myself for the deceit, the corruption, for the facade. Did you ever feel guilty?"

The crook of his right cheek raised and then dropped when he breathed in heavily.

"Yes and no. On the one hand, I didn't care that I built my wealth on a phantom identity. The whole scheme was a passport to anywhere. On the other hand, I always knew I wasn't enough and maybe would never be enough. So I pushed this character as far as it would go, and Donovan fell into my arms. He considered us equals—wealthy, ambitious, conquer-the-world types."

That raw admission, that he didn't hate himself, sat on me like a heavy stone. Nothing turned out as he had hoped. He had wanted Donovan to love him, and he intended on possessing that love like a relic. But now he realized his false self (the only thing he truly possessed) was on life-support—as long as he chased his version of Donovan, he could go on. His biggest misstep was not seeing how extraordinary Donovan was. Jacobi miscalculated what a "worthy boy" like Donovan could do. He disappeared into wealth, into a vibrant life, and left Jacobi with nothing except the feeling of a soul ripped away from its source.

"We met again a few days later. I couldn't breathe. He was so charming, sitting next to me on that wooden swing on his porch. The orange flicker of the bulbs in the lanterns exaggerated his novelty. I remember thinking that I was the one being duped—by his beauty."

Once again, I had gone invisible. Jacobi was speaking, but he had been transported back to that swing.

"Did you just talk, or——?" I tried to return him to me.

"I kissed him. He moaned and pressed into me for more."

Jacobi was gone again, lost in the reverie of youth, and immobilized as though in cryonic suspension—his only way of preserving the mysteries of love, meaning, and his hope for Donovan.

* * *

I got up and went to the kitchen for a drink. When I returned, he didn't seem to notice I'd left.

"I can't explain to you how shocked I was when I realized I'd fallen in love with him, mate. I was almost repulsed. I wanted him to push me away, but he didn't, because he was in love with me as much as I was in love with him. My worldliness took him, but that was fake, too. I simply had had different experiences than him, so I knew different things. We met again and again, and each time I realized I was out of my depth, but I was falling more in love with him every minute. I don't know when it happened, but I just stopped caring."

"Stopped caring about what?" I asked.

"I gave up trying to truly become the man I had pretended to be. Why should I expend the energy doing extraordinary things when all I had to do to seduce him was just talk about what I intended to do?"

"It takes a long time to become real," I said.

"What's that, mate?"

"The Velveteen Rabbit. That's you."

On the last afternoon, before Jacobi went on an extended trip to Europe and Asia, he held Donovan for a long time. Neither spoke. They sat by the fireplace, their cheeks rosy from the warmth. Donovan twisted his body around to kiss Jacobi, and he stroked Donovan's dark hair. They were rehearsing for the time when they would be apart, learning how to live without each other, and delaying the emptiness by bringing it into the fullness of their love. They had never been so intimate as they were in that moment, nor had they conveyed such intensity than when Donovan breathed into Jacobi's chest or when he stroked Donovan's palms, making memories to hold them over until Jacobi returned.

* * *

Jacobi was full of ambition while he was overseas, blending and layering vast amounts of money into real estate, banks, and gemstones. His investments were in high demand, and so was his knowledge of hiding money. He became impatient to get home, but he owed a debt of service to many of his supporters. Every text and phone call with Donovan left him feeling more nervous. Donovan didn't understand what was delaying him in Asia. He was lonely, and his parents' pressure to get an education and find a match was mounting. Without Jacobi's presence and reassurance, Donovan's certainty about who he was and what he wanted wavered.

Donovan was nineteen, and his ersatz life was grand with shiny sports cars, the self-important affectation of upper-class friends, and opulent parties whose throbbing beats drowned out his sadness and invited him to consider a new rhythm. All night the clubs exploded with songs about getting rich and being somebody you're not while throngs of people in flannel shirts, blue jeans, and hoodies convulsed on the dance floor covered in glitter. Fresh faces, some sweet, some feverish, drifted in and out of Donovan's house like ambitious dandelion seeds helicoptering in the wind.

Through this lurid cosmos, Donovan recreated himself; he was dating several girls at once and sleeping with more, crashing at dawn, shirtless, wearing unzipped jeans, and drifting away on sex-stained linens. But the quicksilver flow of his life left him desperate for a decision. He craved structure but needed to be squeezed into it through some pressure, whether by love, money, or usefulness.

In the middle of spring, that pressure took the form of Fallon Macandeior. Donovan was flattered by her massive personality and her social stature. There were obstacles, fully disclosed, but they came to an agreement.

The email about their engagement reached Jacobi just as he returned to the States.

* * *

The first light of the sun yawned on Emerald Bluff now, and we went through the house, opening blinds to chase away the darkness. Bees had begun to swarm the garden, and gulls started their fishing on the lake. The breeze was easy and relaxed.

"He never loved her." Jacobi spun around from a window and looked at me as if he dared me to argue. "He was ecstatic about our plans, mate. Fallon slandered me to the point where Donovan became confused and frightened. She made me look like I was a cheap villain. So, of course, he didn't know what to say. He just fell back on what he thought was safe."

He sat down and rubbed his eyes.

"Maybe he loved her for a quick minute when they married. But that only made his love for me even stronger. Don't you see it?"

"I'm not following your thinking there, Oskar."

"At any rate," he said, "it was just out of convenience."

His words struck me as unusual. There was no other way to interpret them except that Jacobi's mind worked overtime to assert a potency in their affair that could only be verified in vague parameters.

As soon as he returned from Asia, he immediately flew to Columbus, but Fallon and Donovan were still on their wedding cruise. He was drawn there to him. He stayed there a week, because of him. He walked along the streets, stopping at their ghost spots to revisit him. Nothing belonged to Jacobi there, for the only one he wished to see was gone. He walked by Donovan's house, the house that had always seemed more vibrant and joyful than the others; in fact, the entire city had held this enchantment for him, but without Donovan, only melancholy remained.

Wanting to leave that place but afraid he hadn't searched hard enough, that somehow he had missed him and was leaving him behind, he retraced his steps one last time. Jacobi remembered everything. The yearning for Donovan's body, mostly, and the need to have him close, the wish to be rejected by him because hoping was unbearable, and there was no joy without him.

He boarded the plane and sat in first class. As it lifted off the runway, cars streamed across the interstate; perhaps some of the people in them had seen Donovan's sunbathed face on a crowded street.

The craft banked away from the sun, giving one last parting goodbye, and the city in which Donovan had lived and breathed vanished below the clouds. Jacobi stretched out his hand as if to pluck a tuft of air to savor something that Donovan had made wonderful. But the plane was too high and too fast, and Jacobi knew that he had lost the sweetest and the best, forever.

We finished breakfast at nine o'clock and went out on the porch. A hint of fall was in the air. The landscaper, the last of Jacobi's former servants, approached the steps.

"Mr. Jacobi, I'm going to drain the pools today. This norther that came in last night is going to bring the leaves down with it. You don't want any clogs."

"Only the freshwater pool today," said Jacobi. "Leave the saltwater a little longer." He looked at me with a bit of mischief. "You know, mate, I haven't used that saltwater pool since you and I—"

I looked at my watch and stood.

"I've got to go to the office."

I didn't want to drive to Austin. I didn't feel like working. What's more, I didn't want to leave Jacobi. I waited with him another hour.

"I'll call you, Oskar."

"Yes, please, mate."

"Around noon," I said.

We walked down the steps.

"I'm expecting Donovan to call today." He watched for my reaction.

"Maybe he will."

Just before I reached my yard, I remembered something and turned back to him.

"They're a shitty bunch," I shouted across the lawn. "You're worth more than every damn one of them put together."

I've always been pleased I told him that. It was the only flattering thing I'd ever said to him because I never trusted him from the beginning. Jacobi tipped his head to think about it and then shot me that beaming and reassuring smile as if we'd been savvy about that truth the whole time. He was gorgeous in his white suit, and I remembered that first night when I came to his mansion three months before. The driveway and gardens were packed with guests who conjectured about his sins—and he had stood on those very steps, hiding his impeccable dream, as he waved them goodbye.

I thanked him for his kindness. He always deserved that. "Goodbye," I told him. "Breakfast was delightful, Oskar."

* * *

At the office, I tried to summarize the issues on the latest campaign, but I fell asleep in my chair, head flat on the desk. My phone buzzed. I shot up, hair soaked with sweat. It was Levi who often called me around this time of day to let me know of his whereabouts; he jaunted from hotel to hotel, Airbnbs, friends' houses, and sometimes unmentionable places. He usually sounded steely and sharp, as if an arrow had flown through the speaker, but this morning he was severe and toneless.

"I left Donovan's house," he said. "I'm in West Austin, and I'm heading to the Domain this afternoon for some shopping."

Leaving Donovan's house was probably the polite thing to do, but now no one was there for Donovan. And Levi was going shopping? His next comment pissed me off.

"You were an asshole to me last night."

"Last night wasn't about you."

Silence. Then: "I'd still like to see you, Carry."

"So I'm not an asshole anymore?"

"You are, but how about I don't go to the Domain, and I go downtown this afternoon?"

"This afternoon is no good."

"Work stuff?" asked Levi. What a wicked mind he had.

"Work stuff," I said.

"Fine."

Any other guy would have rejected *work stuff* and pushed harder. Not Levi. He let it go. In anyone else this neutrality would have meant *I don't want conflict.* For Levi, *work stuff* was an excuse to his advantage—for later—which is why I felt even more pissed, or worse, it might have been desperation. I couldn't tell which.

We stopped speaking, and then he hung up. I didn't care. I couldn't stomach seeing him today and wasn't sure if I ever would again.

I called Jacobi a few minutes later but only got his voicemail. I texted him, but there was no reply. I tossed my phone down and decided I'd try again later. I stared at the screen, trying to make sense of the bullet points I'd typed out earlier. It was twelve o'clock.

***

When I passed the bell tower on the way to work that morning, I avoided looking at it and the Giantess. I figured there would be a morbidly curious crowd in that area with kids searching for blood spots in the street and people telling the story of what happened over and over until it became mythical and then forgotten. This is a good place to go back a bit and tell what went on after we left the salon the night before.

They had trouble finding Liam's brother, Danny. When he finally arrived, he was high on ecstasy. He spoke incoherently, smiled stupidly, and asked again and again why his brother was standing in the street. When they convinced him that Liam had been pronounced dead at the scene and taken away in the coroner's van, he fell into a fetal position and cried. Some kind (or abnormally interested) person drove Danny to the morgue.

New faces appeared at the salon long after midnight while Shyla Kearns rocked herself back and forth on the couch inside. People shuffled into the lobby to peek at her through the door. Eventually, someone shooed everyone away and shut it. Abundio and several others stayed with her until they dropped off from exhaustion one by one. Abundio made a pot of coffee and stayed there with Shyla until morning.

By three o'clock, Shyla's moans turned into lucid talk about the yellow car. She repeated that she knew whom the car belonged to and then revealed that her husband had come back from downtown one night with fingernail scratches down his back.

When she heard herself say this, she flung her head between her knees and resumed bellowing, "Oh, my God! Oh, Lord, no." Abundio was at a loss about how to help her.

"How long have you and Señor Kearns been married, señora? Take deep breaths and tell me about your marriage."

"Twelve years."

"Any children? Come on. Sit up and breathe. Did you have children?"

Shiny black crickets jumped at the windows, and whenever Abundio heard a car on the road, it had the familiar sound of the car that hadn't stopped a few hours before. He didn't want to walk around out front because of the bloodstains, so he paced back and forth between the lobby and the salon. By morning he had memorized every hairdryer, pen, curling iron, and brush. When he wasn't pacing, he sat down next to Shyla to try and calm her down.

"Do you go to church? Maybe now would be a good time for you to speak to a priest. Do you want me to call—"

"I don't go to any church."

"Everybody needs church, Señora Kearns. Did you marry in a church? Did you hear my question?"

"Church was a long time ago."

It took great concentration for her to answer Abundio's questions, and for a moment, she stopped rocking and was quiet. But then the horror returned to her eyes.

"Open that drawer," she said, pointing at a desk.

"Which one?"

"That drawer in that desk."

Abundio opened the drawer. In it was a brand new, expensive dog leash.

"Are you looking for this?" he asked, holding it up.

Shyla started to tremble.

"I found it yesterday. He tried to tell me some story about it, but I knew he was lying."

"Señor Kearns bought it?"

"It was all wrapped up in pretty paper."

"So he bought a leash. Maybe he has a friend who got a puppy, you know? Or maybe he was going to surprise you with a dog."

But apparently, she had heard some of the same explanations from Liam because she started wailing "Oh my God!" again, leaving Abundio speechless.

"Then he killed him," said Shyla. Her mouth fell open like a fresh corpse.

"Who killed him? Who?"

"I can prove it."

"Señora, you're in shock," said Abundio. "You're grief-stricken, and you don't know what you're saying. Have some water and stay calm."

"He murdered my husband."

"The police say it was an accident."

Shyla shook her head violently. She stuck out her jaw and narrowed her eyes. "I know the truth," she said. "I give everybody the benefit of the doubt, sometimes too often, but when I know somethin', I know it. That man in that car killed my husband. He ran out to the street to talk to him, and he ran him down."

Abundio recalled Liam running out into the street, but he had thought Mr. Kearns was trying to escape the fight he and his wife were having.

"What did he want to say to the man, you think?"

"He's a mystery, that one."

She began to rock again, only faster, as though possessed.

"You got a friend I could call for you, Señora Kearns?"

He knew better; Shyla barely had anything to offer her husband. Blue light crept in the window, and Abundio was relieved that dawn would soon come.

Shyla walked to the window and looked out at the homeless camps around the bell tower.

"I talked to my husband very bluntly," she said. "And I warned him that he could fool me, but he couldn't fool the Lord." She pointed to the hotel with the Giantess. "I said to him, 'The Lord knows where you've been and who you've been with. You can trick me, but you can't trick the Lord.'"

Abundio realized she was pointing up at the Giantess.

"The Lord sees everything," said Shyla.

"Señora, that's just a mural." Abundio rubbed his eyes and walked back to the chair. But Shyla pressed her forehead to the window and tapped at the pane with her finger.

* * *

By six o'clock, Abundio had nothing more to give. He was relieved when a car pulled up; it was one of the men from the night before keeping his promise to return in the morning. The man cooked breakfast, but Shyla did not eat. She was calm, so Abundio went home to sleep; he jolted awake four hours later and returned to the garage to find Shyla missing.

Her movements—she was on foot part of the time, and then took an Uber—were later traced to the market district, where she bought a sandwich that she partially ate and a cup of coffee. She continued on to Clarksville. She stopped at a gas station there around noon. Police gathered eyewitness reports along her route—a businessman called 911 about a "deranged lady" who had wandered into traffic. The clerk at the gas station reported a "suspicious person" who demanded cigarettes but claimed she had no money. Shyla took an Uber from Clarksville and asked the driver to drop her off at Bob Wentz Park on Lake Travis.

Based on Abundio's statement in which Shyla had relayed to him she'd seen who had driven the yellow car and "killed my husband," the police supposed she spent hours wandering The Lake looking for the car. But no one in the area saw her, so they wondered if she had some other means of finding out where it was. Around two o'clock, she found her way to Emerald Bluff, where she asked for directions to Jacobi's house. So by that time, she knew Jacobi's name.

* * *

At two o'clock, Jacobi told his butler to stand watch over his phone and to bring it to him if anyone called. He also said under no circumstances should his Bacalar be driven—not even to repair the right bumper. He slipped into his bathing suit and went out to the saltwater pool carrying a Louis Vuitton sling bag. He stopped the landscaper and asked about the large raft that had titillated his guests all summer, and the man helped Jacobi inflate it.

Jacobi tossed the raft into the pool; his first attempt to mount it resulted in a bellyflop, which heaved the raft to the steps.

"Do you need help with that, boss?" asked the landscaper.

"No, I'll get it. But if you see anyone or Mr. Macandeior pulling up, get me immediately. Otherwise, I'd like to be alone."

Jacobi waited for the call. The butler, agitated over the neglect of his other responsibilities, sat by the phone until four—

until it was far too late to matter to Jacobi. I think he knew the call would never come. Perhaps he forgave fate the debt it owed him. And if I'm accurate, then, at last, he experienced the anguish of living the wrong life. All at once, the misery of a life never lived rushed in and cleared his vision. He must have looked up at a sky he'd never seen before and cringed as he realized what a hideous thing light was. A new reality dawned on him, palpable but chimerical, where the dead and the living crossed to and fro between a thin veil, animated by hope.

The landscaper—he was one of Rosenberg's associates—heard two shots. During the investigation, he would say he thought nothing of it when he heard the first. The second sent him running. I drove from the office straight to Jacobi's house and caused a commotion rushing up the front steps, throwing the door wide open. But they all knew. Silently, the butler and I hurried down to the pool.

The brine circulated along the dark tiles in quiet ripples. The raft drifted. A breeze barely disturbed the surface tension, enough to agitate its pointless course against its fallen burden. Blood billowed around Jacobi's head and floated out past the raft, an orange-yellow, as though an artist had trailed a brush of red paint through the water. Organic bits clung to the raft like barnacles. When we tried to lift Jacobi from the water, we saw the lacuna in his skull. The landscaper yelled out that he thought there was a gun at the bottom of the pool.

It was after we pulled Oskar out and laid him on the deck that the butler discovered Shyla's body in the garden, and the symmetry of the destruction was complete.

In the sunshine of summer I ne'er lament,
  Because the winter it cannot prevent;
  And when the white snow-flakes fall around,
  I don my skates, and am off with a bound.
  Though I dissemble as I will,
  The sun for me will ne'er stand still;
  The old and wonted course is run,
  Until the whole of life is done;
  Each day the servant like the lord,
  In turns comes home, and goes abroad;
  If proud or humble the line they take,
  They all must eat, drink, sleep, and wake.
  So nothing ever vexes me;
  Act like the fool, and wise ye'll be!

The Fool's Epilogue, by Johann Wolfgang von Goethe

Chapter Nine

After two years, my memory of that day, and that night and the following day, is a blur of police officers in blue and journalists and news reporters jostling to get in and out of Jacobi's mansion. Police cars were parked at the main gate to keep out the morbid onlookers, but some ambitious types figured out that they could reach Jacobi's house through my yard, and some were able to sneak past the police to photograph the pool. I remember a detective uncovering Shyla's body, studying what was left of her face, and his remark, "Such a tragedy," set the tone for the reports the next morning.

Most of the news correspondents and journalists saw the double suicide as their meal-ticket to fame. They postulated conspiracy theories, commented on circumstantial evidence, or fabricated information to fill in the gaps. When Abundio's testimony at trial cast suspicions on Shyla, I was afraid the truth would be skirted in favor of a love scandal—but when Danny was cross-examined, he swore that Liam had never known Jacobi and neither did Shyla. He testified that his brother and sister-in-law had a happy marriage, were planning on moving to Florida, and he sounded convinced of all this, even if by rehearsal. So Shyla was portrayed as a grief-stricken widow who simply arrived at Jacobi's to torment him by her own death. And the case rested there.

But the immediate and essential matter was Jacobi and him alone. As the news broke of the tragedy, every presumption, every rumor, and every honest question was deferred to me. I couldn't grasp why at first. I had only met him a few months ago. Then as he lay in his mansion motionless and silent, hour by hour, I understood why I was responsible—no one else cared—cared, I mean, to complete the needs of the dead until they enter their final rest.

I called Donovan soon after we found him. I didn't hesitate because I thought he needed to know. But he and Fallon were gone.

"They didn't take their phones?"

"No."

"Did they say when they would return?"

"No."

"Where are they? How can I get in touch with them?"

"I'm not going to tell you."

I wanted someone to be there for him. I started for the room where he lay to reassure him: "I will get someone for you, Oskar. Rest easy. Trust me. I'll get someone for you—" but I stopped myself, for how could I be sure I could deliver on my promise?

I didn't have Gabriel Rosenberg's cell number. The butler searched for it frantically but only found his office number. By the time I had it, it was after five, and no one answered.

"Will you try him again?" urged the butler.

"I've called three times already."

"This is urgent, Mr. Iverson."

"I'm aware. But no one is there."

I went back to the room where Oskar lie in repose wrapped in blankets filled with dry ice (on account of Jewish tradition, there would be no embalming) and saw that it was full of people. I hoped they had come to pay their respects. But they merely drew back the sheet to inspect Jacobi with eyes aghast. His voice protested in my mind: "Do this one thing for me, mate. Get someone for me. Try harder. I can't go through this alone."

The spectators began lobbing questions my way, but I dodged them and went upstairs to rummage through the unlocked drawers of his desk. I'd only heard by way of a rumor that his parents were dead. But there was nothing—only the photograph of Morty Foster, a memento of lost love, staring at me from the wall.

The next morning, I sent the butler to Austin to personally urge Mr. Rosenberg to come to Jacobi's house as soon as possible. I was sure I was wasting the butler's time because I figured Rosenberg would make his way out there as soon as he saw the morning news, just as I was certain Donovan would call any minute. But he did not call. And Rosenberg did not come. No one came except more police and more correspondents, wearing thick make-up, red or blue dresses, and navy suits, all with coiffed hair, cameras, and microphones. The butler was on his way back when Rosenberg texted me:

> Dear Mr. Iverson, this has been the biggest shock of my life. I can't believe it's true. The pain Oskar must have been in should make us all think about our actions. I can't come now, important business. Besides, I don't want to get mixed up in any of this. But if I can do anything later, let me know. I've lost my mind over all this and am helpless. But do keep me posted about the funeral. I have no idea about his family.

Jacobi's phone rang that afternoon, and I hoped it was Donovan, finally. But I heard a man's voice on the other end.

"It's Maccabee…"

"Yes?" I'd never heard the name.

"It's a shitstorm. Get my message?"

"There haven't been any messages."

"That young guy Jimmy got nabbed," he said. "He was

busted in a sting. They got his profile off the web and found out who he was meeting. Go figure, eh? You can't be sure of anything in this town—"

"Hey!" I interrupted. "This isn't Mr. Jacobi. Mr. Jacobi shot himself yesterday."

After a long pause, Maccabee muttered an expletive and hung up.

* * *

It was the third day, and I still had not been able to find a rabbi in Austin to carry out the rites (due to the cause of death). But the butler received a call from Joseph Jakobovits in Minnesota saying that he was at Austin Bergstrom waiting for a cab.

It was Jacobi's father, a stately elderly man, who showed up on Jacobi's steps distraught, wearing on that warm September day a black suit and a white shirt with a torn front pocket. He wept continuously from grief, and when I took the suitcase from his hand, he began yanking bits of hair from his gray beard. I pulled his hands away from his face and led him to a chair in the lounge before he collapsed. I asked the butler to get him something to eat, but he pushed the plate away, spilling the cup of tea onto the floor.

"It's been all over the news," he said. "When I saw it, I packed right away."

"I'm sorry. I didn't know how to get in touch with you."

His eyes passed over the room, seeing the remnants of his son's life.

"He must've gone crazy," he said. "Out of his mind."

"Would you drink some coffee?" I asked.

"I don't want anything, Mr.—"

"Iverson."

"It's not the proper time to eat now. Where do they have Oskar?"

I took him into the room where his son lay and left him alone.

Some reporters managed their way to the front steps again and were peering into the hall; when I told them who had arrived and that we needed privacy, they left, dragging their feet.

After some time, Mr. Jakobovits opened the door and walked out, mouth hanging open, face pale, and eyes wet with tears. He had seen death before, but he had reached an age where it no longer surprised him. When he looked around the hall and at the great rooms and saw the magnitude and splendor of it all, his sorrow mingled with wondrous pride. I walked him upstairs to a bedroom. As he took off his jacket, I told him about the trouble I'd encountered making arrangements for burial.

"I'm out of options, and I don't know what you want, Mr. Jacobi—"

"Jakobovits is *my* name."

"—Mr. Jakobovits. I thought maybe you'd want to take him back up—"

He waved his hand.

"Oskar always loved it better down here. This is where he earned his fame. Were you a friend of my son, Mr.—"

"He was my best friend."

He began to weep again. "He had so much going for him, you know? He was so young and so bright."

He placed his fingers on his temples, and I nodded.

"If he would have chosen to live, he would have had a grand life. He could have even been president. He would have saved this country, don't you think?"

"For sure," I said, trying not to shrug.

He scratched at the embroidered comforter and then pulled it over him and lay down. He fell asleep instantly.

That night a man with a frenetic voice called and said he would not reveal who he was unless I gave my name first.

"This is Carry Iverson," I said.

"Thank God! This is Pfeffer."

I was relieved because he could be another friend at Jacobi's grave. I had decided to call up a few people rather than post anything publicly because I didn't want death-tourists showing up at the funeral. Until now, I hadn't heard back from anyone.

"The funeral is tomorrow at three o'clock," I said. "Please invite anyone who you think might want to attend. Anyone with decency, that is."

"Of course, I will," he sputtered. "But I don't see people very often, but if I do…"

His answer made me suspicious.

"You will be there for sure, yes?"

"I'll try my best. The reason for my call—"

"Just a second," I interrupted. "How about making a commitment to come?"

"Well, you see—the truth is—I'm staying with people up here in Round Rock, and it's expected that I attend their picnic tomorrow. But of course, I'll do what I can to get away."

All restraint left me. "After everything he did for you…"

Pfeffer heard me but kept on nervously. "I called because I left a pair of shoes there. Would you mind having the butler bring them to me? The address I'm at is—"

"Fuck off," I said, and then hung up.

The disgraces only kept piling on. One man I called said that Jacobi did to himself what everyone else wanted to do to him. I should have been more careful because he was one of the party guests who, emboldened by Jacobi's liquor, derided him endlessly. I should have known better.

The morning of the funeral, I drove into Austin to confront Mr. Rosenberg; he wasn't returning my calls or texts. The sign on the door to his office read: Wehrmacht Holding Company. I knocked, but no one came to the door. When I shouted "hello" several times and banged on the door, bickering broke out, and finally, a beautiful Jewish woman opened the door and surveyed me with distrusting brown eyes.

"Nobody's here," she said. "And Mr. Rosenberg is in Dallas."

Obviously, it wasn't true that no one was there. She was, and whoever was whistling inside the office.

"Please, tell Mr. Rosenberg that Mr. Iverson needs to speak with him."

"You want that I should flap my arms to Dallas and carry him back here with me?"

"Ruth!" yelled Mr. Rosenberg from the other side of the door.

"Leave your name and number on the pad," she said. "And I'll make sure he sees it when he gets back."

"But he's in there!"

She stepped toward me and slid her hands into her blouse.

"You young people think you can push us old folks around," she said. "And we've had it." She shoved my chest feebly. "So when I tell you he's in Dallas, he's in Dallas!"

"This is about Mr. Jacobi."

"Jacobi!" She looked me up and down again. "Just stay right—what's your name again?"

She closed the door. The sound of her heels clopped across the floor.

In a few seconds, Gabriel Rosenberg opened the door and put his arm around me, leading me into his office.

"We're all mourning him. It's such a loss," he said. "Cigar?"

I sat down and shook my head.

"I'll never forget when I first met him. He was so ambitious and had a mind for our kind of work. He was street smart. He learned a lot from Foster and his travels. But he wasn't the refined Jacobi that you know. Knew. The first time I saw him was when he came into Player's poolroom on Guadalupe. I walked right up to him and said, 'Hey handsome, have lunch with me.'"

"Did you get him started in the business?" I asked.

"Get him started? I made the man."

"I see."

"I took in that diamond in the rough because I saw beneath the crust there was a gentleman and a cutthroat businessman. When he told me he went to Harvard, I knew he was just what we were looking for. I got him into the Masons, and he shot right up the ladder. He did a job for a client of mine in Houston. I was impressed. Soon we were as thick as thieves, and we never left each other's side."

I got the feeling this "business" Rosenberg was referring to involved fixing deals and dirty money.

"And now he's dead," I said. "You were his mentor and friend, so you must come to his funeral this afternoon."

"Believe me; I want to come."

"Then come. If you loved him, you'll come."

His eyebrows touched when he frowned. He shook his head, and his eyes filled with tears.

"I just can't. I can't get mixed up in this," he said.

"Mixed up in what? Everything ended with Jacobi."

"When someone dies, I don't get involved in any way. I keep far from it. When I was younger, I felt differently. If a friend died, it didn't matter how he went; I was with him to the end. That may sound schmaltzy to you, but that was what I did."

I was fighting a losing battle. I stood to leave.

"Did you graduate from college?" he asked.

I was appalled to think he would suggest a deal to me now, but he only nodded and shook my hand.

"Take some advice. Give your flowers to the living, don't wait until they're dead. Beyond that, leave everything else alone."

When I left Rosenberg's office, the sky had turned dark, and it began to rain as I drove back to Emerald Bluff. I changed into a suit and went next door. Mr. Jakobovits was pacing in the hall. When he saw me, he walked out to the driveway. From the look of him, his respect for his son and his gratification in his son's possessions had grown twofold.

"I need to show you something," he said.

He took out his wallet, fingers trembling. "Oskar sent me this picture. Look."

It was a photograph of Jacobi's mansion, creased and covered in fingerprints.

"Look at that grand doorway. And the landscaping. Can you imagine?"

He looked into my eyes, expecting me to be as proud as he was. He had looked at that picture so often, I think it was more real to him than the mansion itself.

"Oskar sent it to me. It's such a beautiful picture. It speaks so well of him."

"It's a beautiful place. When was the last time you saw him?" I asked.

"He came to Minnesota a couple of years ago. He bought me the house I live in now. We were devastated when he left home, but I understand it now. He had to chase his dream, his bright future. And when he made it, he was very kind to me."

Jakobovits held on to the photograph, hesitating to put it away. He held it up for me again and smiled. Then he put it in his wallet and took out a small Moleskine notebook.

"Take a look at this. It was a little day planner from when he was a boy. Proof of a genius."

I opened it to the first page where Jacobi had written SCHEDULE and the date September 4, 2001. And underneath:

Wake up	6:00 a.m.
Parkour	6:15-6:45 a.m.
Study math, etc.	6:45-7:30 a.m.
School	7:30-3:30 p.m.
Sports	4:00-5:00 p.m.
Memory skills	5:00-6:00 p.m.
Plan Inventions	7:00-9:00 p.m.

RULES

* Do not waste time at the arcade or with William
* Do not smoke or drink
* Take a bath every day
* Brush teeth every day
* Read one self-help book a week
* Save ~~$20~~ $10 a week
* Treat parents with respect

"I found it by accident," said Jakobovits. "Proof, right?"

"Yes, proof."

"Oskar was destined to make something of himself. He always had rules like this and manifestos. Notice how much of his time he's dedicated to improving his mind. He couldn't get enough of that. One time he told me my mind was getting dull, and I spanked him for it."

Again, he didn't want to close the book. He read each item to me and kept looking at me with such earnestness as if he wanted me to write down Jacobi's list for my own self-improvement.

The rabbi from the reform synagogue in Austin arrived just before three, and I began watching nervously for other cars. Jacobi's father joined me. Time passed. The butler, the landscaper, and a few other staff came in and stood in the hall. Mr. Jakobovits squinted his eyes, searching for more cars.

"The rain might delay people," he said.

"Could be."

The rabbi checked her watch several times, so I took her aside and asked her to wait another half hour. But it was pointless. No one else came.

* * *

About five o'clock, we stood to carry Jacobi to his grave in the garden. Because of the suicide, he was not permitted to be buried in a Jewish cemetery—not that I think he would have cared. Mr. Jakobovits and I, the butler and the landscaper, and a few staff gathered around the casket. As we started to lift it, I heard a car pull in the driveway and then the sound of squeaky shoes running toward us. I turned around. It was the man with raven eyes whom Levi and I had met analyzing Jacobi's books in the library one night three months ago.

Since then, I had not run into him, and I don't know how he knew about the funeral. I didn't even know his name. He wiped down his hair and eyes and looked at the coffin.

I tried to focus on Jacobi for a moment, but he already felt so far from me, and then I realized, with some bitterness, that Donovan hadn't called or texted or even sent a damn flower. Faintly I heard raven-eyes say, "Blessed be the one true judge," and Mr. Jakobovits whispered, "Amen."

We carried Jacobi down the front steps. We paused, and the rabbi read a section of Psalm 91: "He who dwells in the shelter of the Most High, who abides in the shadow of the Omnipotent…" We took a few more steps and stopped again: "The Lord who is my refuge and my stronghold, my God in whom I trust…" The rain had become a deluge now, and by the time we reached the pool, we were all wet to the skin: "He will save you from the ensnaring trap, from the destructive pestilence…" We had to walk and then stop four more times according to tradition. When we reached the grave, the rabbi recited from memory: "When he calls on me, I will answer him; I am with him in distress, I will deliver him and honor him. I will satisfy him with long life and show him my deliverance." Raven-eyes tore a corner of his front pocket. We took turns shoveling dirt over the casket, and the final prayers were recited.

As we sloshed our way back to the house, raven-eyes held my arm.

"I got here!" he said.

"You did. Thank you very much."

"A shame! My God, boy! They used to come here by the hundreds.

He wiped his hair and eyes again.

"God pities an imposter," he said.

* * *

I vividly remember coming home from prep school and college for Christmas break. The peacoats of the boys and the chattering teeth in the frozen air and the greetings by old friends, and the comparing of invitations: "I'm going to a party at the Delaney's," "I'll be at the Wechsler's," "Are you going to the Klerkens? Me, too!" And our gloved hands, which were never warm enough, but still we insisted on waiting outside for our parents to pick us up by the gate.

When we drove out into the winter night, and the Ohio snow remade the world into an enchanted, glittering snow globe, and the faint lights of Ohio towns passed by, an untamed crackle crystalized the air. We couldn't breathe it in fast enough as we walked to the doors of our homes, hungry for dinner. We were conscious of our unity with this land for one magic moment, and then we melted into it again, no longer keen to its freshness.

That's my Ohio—not the cornfields or the forests or the Amish villages, but the fresh returning snow of my youth, the Christmas lights in the square and the sleigh bells in the wintry night and the noble trees decorated and lit in the windows. I belong to that. Sure, it's a little melancholy when the winters stretch long. And I'm a touch smug from growing up an Iverson. But I understand, after all this time, that this has really been a story about my roots, after all—Fallon and Jacobi, Donovan and Levi and I were all Midwesterners, and maybe we were all flawed in the same way that made living anywhere else uninhabitable.

But Austin wounded me. It broke me by my incongruous need for wholesomeness and passion. It maimed me by that carnal dance of false nostalgias and plangent remorse.

Austin. The city that was to be my new beginning but became the womb that miscarried a self I thought I wanted to be and maybe should have become but never did; a self I left for dead and would never do a thing again to resurrect.

Even when Austin excited me most, even when I could see the advantages over the dull, bloated towns of Ohio, with their nosy neighbors and gossipy pastimes—even then, Austin was alien to me. The Hollows, especially, haunt me. Visions rise in my dreams like a series of Evard Munch's paintings: rows of mansions dripping like wax with gaunt and sullen men and women roaming the streets under a dark moon. In the foreground stands a nude woman, but she is dead, her body adorned with bracelets and necklaces, and she is being serenaded by a cadaver-like man playing the guitar. Passersby don't look at either of them. They don't care.

After Jacobi's suicide, Emerald Bluff was haunted, too, warped beyond repair. So when the trees shed their leaves, and the grass (Jacobi's and mine) had finally withered, I decided to return to Oberlin.

I had just one thing to wrap up. One awkward and disagreeable thing—and had I remembered Rosenberg's advice, I would have left it alone. But leaving it undone would have added to my misery later. I called Levi and asked him to stop by. We sat apart on the couch, and he listened.

"I didn't want to leave and sweep everything we went through under the rug," I said.

He didn't move.

"The way I left things with you—I regret."

"You just dropped me, Carry."

"I know. And I'm sorry. When Jacobi—"

"Don't use Jacobi as your scapegoat. You couldn't accept me and what I am, and that's what it's all about."

He was dressed in a sports coat and khakis. I remember thinking he looked like a model, his chin raised dashingly, his hair now highlighted in auburn, his face the same brown hue of his gloves resting on his knee.

"Maybe. But I was trying. It was all new to me, and I had mixed feelings about a lot of things," I said.

"You were in love with Jacobi," he said. "But that's no excuse for dropping me. But it doesn't matter anyway. I'm engaged to a man who *does* know what he wants."

I didn't believe him, although there were several he could have married at the nod of his head, but I pretended to be happy for him. Doubt crossed my mind for a second. *Was I making a mistake?* But then I quickly thought it all through again and got up to say goodbye.

"I don't give a fuck about you now, Carry, but you were entertaining for a while."

We shook hands.

"And darling, you remember that talk we had about my driving?" he asked.

"Not really."

"You asked me what would happen if I came across a driver as offensive as me. Well, I guess I did." He looked me right in the eyes. "I got you all wrong, and that's on me. Because I thought you were honest and sincere like you cared about those things."

"I'm twenty-five," I said. "I'm a decade too old to lie to myself and call it respectable."

He didn't respond. Irritated, and half in love with him, and remorseful, I turned away.

* * *

One afternoon in late October, I ran into Fallon Macandeior. She was walking ahead of me on Congress Avenue in her hurried and aggressive way, one hand in front of her body ready to push aside a slow walker, head darting from side to side, as though it were trying to keep pace with her searching eyes. I slowed down to avoid catching up to her, but she stopped to look in the window of an antique store. She saw me out of the corner of her eye and walked toward me. She thrust out her obligatory hand, and I stared at it.

"What's the matter, Carry? Too good to shake my hand?"

"Yes, and you know why."

"You should see a therapist, Carry." She said my name harshly. "You're fucked up. I don't know what's happened to you."

"Fallon, what did you say to Shyla that afternoon?"

She stared at me with an expressionless face, and I knew I had pieced together what happened during those missing hours. I turned to walk away, but she moved in quickly and snatched my arm.

"What did I say? I told her everything. She showed up at the house while we were packing to leave. I told my secretary to inform her that we weren't there, but she pushed her way in and started to head upstairs. She was crazed and mad enough, and I was afraid she would kill us all. She had a gun, Carry! So I had to tell her the car was Jacobi's."

Fallon folded her arms, satisfied with her explanation. "And it wouldn't have mattered who told her what. Jacobi checked himself out. You and Donovan may have been under his spell, but I knew he was a killer all along. He ran down Liam and then killed himself—what a limp-wristed coward!"

I had nothing left to say to her except the one truth I would never tell.

"And one more thing," she said. "You aren't the only one suffering here. When I went to end the lease on my apart—our apartment and found that fucking box of dog treats sitting on the counter where Liam had left them, I lost it, Carry. I'm not a crier, but I couldn't help myself. There was no damn good reason for what Jacobi did. He was a monster."

I would never forgive Fallon, and I nearly hated her, but I understood how she was able to do what she did, as despicable as it was. It was reckless and illogical. But that's how they lived, Fallon, Donovan, and Levi; they were reckless people who stole wealth and decimated lives and then fell back on their fortunes and status, or whatever it was that quilted them together and let others clean up their shit.

I forced myself to shake her hand; because at that moment, I saw through her mask and understood I had been dealing all along with a dangerous child. She smirked and went inside the antique shop, maybe to buy old jewelry, or perhaps a pair of scissors, to remove the patch of my narrow-minded worldview from their precious quilt forever.

* * *

Jacobi's mansion, now fallen into desuetude, had been cleared out when I left. The shrubbery in front of the house was wild, and his gardens had withered. Rough brown leaves covered the lawn. One of the ride-share drivers from the area never missed an opportunity to pass the entrance gate and point inside, telling the story of the magical and tragic life of Oskar Jacobi. Maybe he had been the driver who took Donovan and Jacobi over to The Hollows the night of the accident, or perhaps he made up the story as he went. I made a point to never ride with him because I couldn't bear to hear another tale.

I stayed in Austin on the weekends because of the ghosts at Jacobi's house. Vivid in my mind was the DJ who rocked the garden, the weird postures of the silver neon-haired twins, the vibrant dancing and drunken laughter, the cars coming in and out of his driveway. One night I did see an actual vehicle at the gate; its lights focused on everything dead. But I kept away. Whoever it was, maybe a final guest who hadn't heard because they had been party-crashing elsewhere, soon figured out the party was over.

On my last night, having sold the SUV and given Achilles up for rehoming, I walked over and stared at that unfathomable disaster of a house one last time. Across each white marble step, someone had scribbled ROT IN HELL FAGGOT LOSER with a garishly pink marker. It seemed to glow in the moonlight. I tried to scrub it clean but only managed to smear a few letters. I followed the path down to the cove and stretched out on the sand.

Most restaurants and cafes were closed now, and the lake was nearly dark except for the blinking red lights of the cell towers atop the shadowy hills and the liquified, lubricious reflections of houses near the shores.

As the moon made her ascent and my eyes adjusted to the growing darkness, the boundaries of things seemed to disappear. I became aware of the tiny Monkey Island, an archipelago that was at one time a steep hill and part of the vibrant ecosystem of the Texas Hill Country until Mansfield Dam was constructed on the Colorado River in 1940, creating Lake Travis. Its drowned cliffs, made from the same stone that fortified Jacobi's mansion, had once inspired the greatest—and maybe the most honest—human emotion: awe, which takes our breath away and invites us to investigate the outrageous frailty of our existence.

And as I sat there on the beach, contemplating this passing stage of my life, I thought of Jacobi's amazement when he first viewed the copper statue of Apollo on the hill of Donovan's land. Jacobi had fought his way through hell to end up here—his Eden—and his dream must have felt so imminent that he never imagined it might fail. He didn't understand that it had already passed him by, lost somewhere in the obscurity of time, where illusions and devils danced under the night sky.

Jacobi had faith in Apollo, charging the morning sun with his chariot, and in that furious bliss of a future, that day by day ebbs away. It eluded Apollo today, but never mind—tomorrow he will charge faster, stretch out his arms further…and one bright morning—

So we push on, sails against the wind, hoisted back endlessly into the past.

A Note About The Author

Akiva Hersh earned his degrees in neurolinguistics and theology. He writes novels about LGBTQ+ issues, sexuality, and relationships. His debut novel *Boy in the Hole* was released in 2019 on National Coming Out Day. Publishers Weekly called it "heartfelt" and "emotionally affecting." The book received five stars from Readers' Favorite.

When not writing Literary Fiction, Akiva pens short stories and poems, hikes with his insane but devoted Miniature American Shepherd, Zeke, plays classical piano and enjoys suspense/horror flicks.

The Magus and The Fool
By Akiva Hersh
Reading Group Guide

The Magus and The Fool is an ideal novel for reading groups. It raises issues about class distinctions, homophobia, transphobia, racism, and love, among many other problems.

This is my guide for reading groups, but spoiler alert: If you haven't yet read the novel, the guide gives away aspects of the plot.

All the best,
Akiva Hersh

1. Since I began writing, I have wanted to give a classic novel a makeover, a Queer retelling, specifically. When *The Great Gatsby* was released into the public domain, I felt it was a perfect choice because the themes F. Scott Fitzgerald explored in 1924 are still relevant today.

    What is class distinction? Do you think it still exists in America? Why or why not?

2. The narrator, Carry Iverson, mentions that he leaves Oberlin, Ohio, because he "became anxious and ill at ease with the Midwestern pace of life." What do you think was behind his anxiety and discomfort?

    Have you ever moved away from a place for similar reasons? What were you hoping would change?

3. Carry works for a social justice firm as a campaign director. At his first dinner with Fallon, Donovan, and Levi, Fallon launches into a racist rant. Neither Carry nor the rest of the group confronts Fallon directly. What would you have done if you had been in Carry's shoes?

4. In chapter two, Carry tells us about The Giantess overlooking the bell tower surrounded by homeless encampments. What does this juxtaposition represent? Do any of the characters have an obligation to help the plight of the homeless?

5. At the party in Fallon's apartment in downtown Austin, Danny (Liam's brother) tells Carry, "The only thing those two have in common is they both hate who they're married to." He was referring to Liam and Fallon. How does this insight affect your perception of Liam and Fallon?

   Do you have empathy for them? Why or why not?

6. What is your impression of Carry by the end of chapter two? How does he compare to the people in his new life?

7. Gossip is the life-blood of the relationships for most people in *The Magus and The Fool*. One wonders what they would talk about if they weren't gossiping about someone else! Why do people gossip? Does any good come from it?

8. In chapter four, there is a long list of Jacobi's party guests. What function does this serve in the novel?

9. In chapter five, Carry and Jacobi go for a night swim. What are Jacobi's motives? Is he attracted to Carry?

10. What kind of work do you think Jacobi has in mind for Carry?

11. What internal struggle is Carry having regarding his relationship with Levi?

    Is it transphobic if a cisgender male who is gay chooses not to date a transman?

    Why did Carry break off his relationship with Levi?

    Do you think Carry accepts his sexuality?

    How would you characterize Donovan's sexuality?

12. What was the nature of the relationship between Carry Iverson and Morty Foster?

13. If the novel came to a close at the end of chapter seven, how would you rewrite it?

14. Jacobi was obsessed with a life that could have been but no longer was and felt that fate owed it to him, so he could never let it go. This was Jacobi's version of hope. Have you held on to a could-have-been life

or self? Is this hope? If not, what is the remedy?

15. Why did Oskar Jacobi and Shyla Kearns take their own lives? Contrast the possible differences in their motives for committing suicide. What other choices did they have?

CPSIA information can be obtained
at www.ICGtesting.com
Printed in the USA
LVHW012011230622
721998LV00002B/128